Steele Mackaye

Investigations

The Tarot Problem

by

Barry H. Wiley

www.creatorofmysteriousstories.com

ISBN 978-0692452073

ISBN 0692452079

"Always good to work with a man who appreciates the need for anonymity in this kind of endeavor".

Remington Steele

1982

The Tarot Problem

1

His name tonight was Steele Mackaye, pronounced mah-*kai* with the emphasis on the second syllable. Tomorrow night his name would be Sam Milliron, pronounced mill-iron with the emphasis on Sam. Tonight he was supporting a charity sponsored by the Mystery Writers and Readers Association of which he had been an active member for several years. Tomorrow night, he would be signing his latest book on Polynesian religions, *The Coming of 'Oro,* at the Los Angeles Natural History Museum at a charity dinner to save black rhinos or the Loch Ness Monster, it didn't seem to matter. One night fiction, the next truth. Fiction paid better than truth as any politician, certainly in California, would quietly tell you with some confidence.

Dark haired, long, wavy, with … blue eyes. She was quite attractive, conservatively dressed in dark pink, and preoccupied as she settled into the chair next to Mackaye. Remember that second syllable. Three other seats were already filled, leaving one empty chair at the table. There were about forty tables arranged in concentric arcs with a speaker's podium at the focus. This was at the Airport Marriott on Century.

"Sorry your husband couldn't make it. Hope he isn't too ill," said Mackaye, raising his glass of passable zinfandel. A shot of sharp pain suddenly went through his left knee, a recurrent long ago football memory. He gritted his teeth, then it was gone.

Yes, they were blue, a haunting blue, and her eyebrows were raised as she turned to him. "How …?"

"You're married, the ring … the chair next to you is still empty though dinner started ten minutes ago … and no husband worth his salt would let you out alone to a meeting like this unless he was sick in bed."

Her laugh was pleasant and brief. She extended her hand. "I'm Elizabeth Vaughn. And, yes, my husband, Jim, is sick in bed. He told me to get out and let him sleep. I had earned some free time. So, here I am."

Her fingers were long, graceful and her grip solid, a business grip.

"I'm Steele Mackaye. I belong here, but I haven't seen you at any of the regular gatherings of the MWRA. Your husband a member?"

She nodded as she swallowed her ice water. "He loves mysteries and mystery writers. He prefers the classics, Hammett, Wilkie Collins, Ross MacDonald, to the political correctness and unimaginative violence of so many of the current writers" A quick half-smile. "He does use a much briefer description some of the modern product." Mackaye's hair was gray at the temples, she noted, no wedding ring, but there had been once, a pleasant though not handsome face with some wear evident. An honest smile. About 60, she would estimate.

"Political bullshit, perhaps?" offered Mackaye. One of the ladies two chairs beyond gave him a withering dirty look at his verbal transgression.

Elizabeth grinned. "You get the idea. The odd thing is that Jim likes mysteries, but I really don't. I'm a private investigator and my mysteries are the real thing. I don't need to waste my time reading about phony ones, even what he assures me are the classics." She sipped more ice water and jabbed once or twice at the charity salad. "I have one mystery, however, that is really giving me trouble, which, given your accurate deductions, must be obvious."

"The talks aren't going to launch for a bit, Elizabeth, so if talking it out would be of any help, my ears are open and my mouth closed."

The salads were being collected in preparation for the promised Cajun-rubbed organic wild-caught suitably-sedated salmon dinner as Elizabeth took a deep breath, then looked up at the waitress approaching. The waitress nodded to her direction and disappeared. She returned a moment later with a filled wineglass of the evening's red.

"So," Mackaye said, sipping again, "how long have you been a PI?"

She swallowed then replaced the glass. "Acceptable, but definitely not great." Wiping a napkin across her lips, Elizabeth Vaughn said, "Seven and a half years; three with my own firm. Along with the usual M.A. in Criminal Justice … and an undergrad degree in physics. And no, I am not packing." Her mouth twisted in disgust, she rotated the stem of the wine glass at her fingertips. "As soon as people, particularly men, find out I'm a PI that is the first dumb question they ask. Too many ignorant PI shows on television."

"Where are you located?

"Burbank."

"Too few clients?"

"Too many actually, about three too many; three who have become the heart of my positive cash flow. They are satisfied with my firm's casework, but they are hesitant about increasing my case load as I am too far away from their main offices for the personal consultations needed for their big cases … and they want me to add at least one more experienced operative. None of the three want to be the difference between my success … or bankruptcy. They want to see me doing more with more."

"Where are they, the key three?"

"Around Century City, while I am on the other side of the moon in Burbank." She sighed, and began to unload, what the hell. "And my lease is up in a month; and I need to find more space to add probably at least two more operatives, one at least who speaks Chinese; and to subscribe to two new very expensive search databases, and," she shrugged, "some other … lesser things."

"Do you have the operatives you need identified?" said Mackaye, an idea warming in his mind.

Elizabeth studied Steele Mackaye. "You do deductions, but I'm the private detective. What do you do, Steele? And yes, I know who I would hire in a minute, if other things worked out."

He handed her his card from a leather holder.

"Steele Mackaye Investigations, LLC?" She frowned. "You are a PI?"

"No. When I retired from the high-tech global game almost nine years ago I starting writing, something I've always wanted to do. I love history, so I write historical mystery fiction as Steele Mackaye, with some modest success; and historical non-fiction as my real name, Sam Milliron, with some of the usual initials attached, as necessary. My investigations are historical, whether public or private."

"I gave you my card, Elizabeth, to suggest an address."

Elizabeth noted: Suite 1157, Century Park Plaza, 2029 Century Park East, Century City 90067. It was only three blocks from her largest client, Delta Blue Asset Management, and about four or five blocks from her other two key clients. She looked up frowning and started to ask ...

"If it fits your schedule, drop by Friday any time after eight o'clock. My coffee will beat anything you have ever tasted. It is not PI coffee." Steele grinned and put out his hand. "I also have one or two databases you might find of interest, along with a tenacious research associate with a great sense of humor, who knows how to find almost anything.

"And I'm not packing either."

Elizabeth Vaughn took his extended hand, held it for a moment, her lips parted in a half-smile, which slowly widened. She nodded and squeezed.

The politely inconvenienced salmon arrived on schedule, glistening red ... and, of necessity, politically green.

2

"It was enchanting, Boss, their birthdates were identical … identical! It *had* to be the gods, maybe even 'Oro himself," said Moana, her golden face flushed with excitement. "I just know it was."

Mackaye leaned back in his chair. Moana's excitement was always charming and always enriched his day. But …

"How big a party was it, Moana?" he asked, as the remarkably attractive Polynesian woman gathered up the notes from their regular Friday morning project status meeting.

She paused. "A big one, I think, 25 … maybe 30 people." Her excitement began to fade. Moana had experienced this before, that calming tone of voice, not suspicious, just so unnaturally calm. How could such a marvelous man have such a … a granite mind?

"I trust their relationship, Moana, will thrive because of circumstances other than the paranormal. The odds of two people meeting at a party with the identical birthdate are 50-50 if there are at least 23 people present. The more people, of course, the better the odds."

"Not paranormal, not the will of the gods … just the damn odds?" All excitement was gone. Then a brilliant, triumphant smile flashed across her face. "But they are going out tonight, to the Polo Lounge, birthdates or not."

Mackaye laughed. "Remember Moana, we only do truth on Monday, Wednesday and Fridays; we are paranormal on Tuesdays and Thursdays." With a shy grin, Moana turned as Mackaye also heard the office door open in the waiting area.

Moana walked quickly out of his office, closing the door firmly behind her. It was too early for the mail delivery.

Mackaye turned back to the computer screen, frowning. Even with his growing status in the mystery field, *Ellery Queen Mystery Magazine* had just rejected his story, "Darknot", because though the story was "compelling and innovative", the language was "too severe" for their readers. He hit a few more keys to send the story to London for inclusion in an anthology of paranormal mysteries.

Would pay better, too.

***

Elizabeth Vaughn walked rapidly down the black granite and white-walled corridor dodging among the hurriedly moving people focused on getting to work. She was dressed in PI formal for a client status meeting at 10:30 at 1901 Avenue of the Stars, a relatively short walking distance away from the twin triangular Century Plaza Towers. Jim had finally succeeded in pulling her into bed from working at her charts at one in the morning. But the charts that graphically laid out the data leaks were solid, conclusive – as were the names of the three leakers. Michael Zenner, her top operative would be there twenty minutes ahead of her with the Powerpoints, the photos, and the tracking discs. Almost four months of heavy investigative effort … but a well-paid effort.

PI formal was a dark green silk suit with a black silk scarf with low heels -- her running shoes, as she thought of them. And no, she wasn't packing. Elizabeth grinned. And neither had been Steele Mackaye. And yes, she remembered the second syllable. She passed another glass-doored empty space which displayed the floor-to-ceiling windows in each office. She liked Mackaye, liked his presence.

Since getting off the elevator and turning the corner of the triangular floor there had been three other empty offices with wooden doors, even though the black granite floor of the main lobby below had echoed with traffic. A central grassy park framed by the vast glass wall of the lobby had looked inviting … maybe for writing poetry someday.

There it was: Steele Mackaye Investigation, LLC, painted in red in an inverted trapezoid on the double glass door. 1157 was also in red. She could see an unoccupied receptionist desk as she pushed the door open. The office decorations seemed vaguely familiar: The red doors leading off the reception area; the tall glass vase of birds-of-paradise sitting on a red ledge projecting out from the wall like a peninsula; the overstuffed chairs and couch. But then, a large utterly captivating painting hanging on the wall behind the desk: an enthralling tropical island valley with two stark green mountains jutting up from the jungles into wisps of low hanging clouds. Clearly not a cliché … it was the real thing.

"To oe faearaa," said the smiling face and glistening dark eyes of the extraordinary black-haired woman walking

toward her with a rhythmic sway to her hips. The woman raised her hand. "May you live," she repeated. "Ms Vaughn?"

"Yes. May I live?"

"I am Moana. My greeting is from my island of Mo'orea, from many generations of my people. The boss is on a short unexpected conference call, but he asked me to show you around. But first I am to get you a cup of real coffee, not PI coffee. I know what that tastes like." Her sour expression triggered laughter from both women. "You are looking at my island, there on the wall. This way please, Ms Vaughn."

"I am Beth, Moana. Your greeting is so charming. I would love to learn more of Moorea. Did I say that right?"

"Almost, Beth. It is Mo'orea. The glottal stop is like one of the letters in our alphabet. We have only thirteen letters in our language … so we need all the help we can get," said Moana, laughing. "This way to the coffee … then on to the badlands."

***

Mackaye looked up as the door pushed open. Two remarkably attractive women walked in with one carrying his steaming morning cup. Not even heaven had perks like this.

"Please excuse me, Beth. Boss, there is that letter to our favorite publisher that needs another draft." A quick nod to Steele's quick thumbs up, Moana was gone, silently.

Mackaye followed Elizabeth's eyes settling behind him as she sat down. It was a large broken piece of ceramic centered on the wall behind him. It was painted rose-red across about a third of the piece with a woman standing at a railing with a tea cup in her hand.

"That is a Roman coffee break circa 14 A.D. The original is in the Getty Villa Museum. What do you think, Elizabeth, after your trek through our badlands?"

She noted the arched polished steel desk lamp with a small analog clock in the base. Still familiar. "Moana is one of the most charming people I have ever met, Steele. And the offices, meeting room, and your broadband capabilities with those databases -- I can only dream of that." She shrugged. "Perfect, in other words."

"When would you like to move in?" Mackaye sipped, then leaned forward to slide a sheet of paper toward her. "Under one of those conditions."

"The layout *is perfect*, but I could never afford the overhead in this tower. It is not a PI-friendly location."

Mackaye pointed at the paper. "Read the conditions of occupancy -- in the expensive words of my lawyer who lives two floors below us."

Placing her cup on the koa wood sidetable next to her chair, Vaughn read the page, her eyebrows rising. After a few moments, she looked up. "This is for real?" She tapped the paper.

Steele nodded. "Almost six years ago when I had outgrown my space at home and realized I needed more office space with room enough for a research associate if I was ever to finish another book, I picked the towers since they would be convenient for a number of reasons. The office occupancy rate at that time in this, the north tower, was way down, so I did a deal with the then tower management. Tower management changed since then.

"This tower of 44 floors had sixteen floors completely empty at the time, with additional vacancies on other floors.

So, I agreed to take space on one of the empty floors at a discount, agreed to pay upfront the first two years of a six year lease with a two-year optional renewal at the same rates, also at further discount, and finally obtained this suite of offices of about three times the space I actually needed." He shrugged. "You never know what the future may require. My lease rate for the next few years is comfortably south of $2.80 a square foot, while the going current rate is about $5.00 and climbing."

"So, yes it is real. You can move in immediately as just a sub-leased tenant at $500 a month; or, as the paper suggests in a couple of steps, merging your operation with my legal structure which would certainly simplify your financial setup. You, under that scenario, would become executive VP and director of investigative operations of Steele Mackaye Investigations, LLC."

Elizabeth Vaughn bit her lip, slowly shaking her head. A near perfect setup. Only because Jim had been sick and she had gone to that boring writers' dinner anyway. The hands of Moana's gods for sure, one of them at least. "Yes, I could start moving in on the weekend, as a tenant. No first and last?"

Mackaye shook his head, laughing. "Nah, you look trustworthy. Let's get some more coffee. There some more stuff you should know.

"The first of which," he said, pushing back his koa wood chair, "is that Moana has a Ph.D. in Polynesian anthropology from the University of Hawai'i, the Manoa campus. Behind that marvelous smiling face is a very sharp-edged intelligence. Moana is fluent in languages that only the gods remember. And," he grinned, "you never want to provoke her by calling her Doctor. She detests academic bureaucracy."

Elizabeth was in a daze as she passed through the red door. Almost oppressed with worries and issues when she arrived, but now almost giddy with relief.

***

As she wedged into the tight people-salad in the elevator to start down the eleven floors, she suddenly realized why Steele Mackaye's office had looked so familiar. With its red doors and interior decorations, it looked almost like the office of *Remington Steele*, the old detective show from the 80's. It had been the Laura Holt character in that show which had first triggered in Elizabeth the idea of maybe being a private eye.

Even though the reruns of the show she'd watched had only been fantasy, it had made the choice of a career become real and personal for Elizabeth.

She chuckled as the elevator doors slid open and everyone could breathe out. Now, she would be working in Remington Steele's office. Elizabeth walked across the lobby laughing softly.

It was crazy… Just crazy.

May you live. Yes, yes … *may you live.*

3

"I was delighted to learn of your pending change of address, Ms Vaughn. That makes you a close neighbor," said James Kennedy, chairman of the board of Delta Blue Asset Management. Kennedy had asked to speak with her in private following their scheduled meeting.

The morning status meeting had gone very well, with the president of Delta Blue, Max Buckminster, saying that with the evidence presented that morning they would take over now from her firm to bring the difficult and embarrassing situation to a resolute conclusion, which, he had added after getting a nod from Kennedy, whose pale paunchy face was drawn tight, which would, Buckminster emphasized with his fist, include the police as appropriate.

"According to our internal reckoning, the successful resolution of this case will save Delta Blue close to $4 million this year. So Ms Vaughn, you will find in the final numbers" – Buckminster withdrew an envelope from inside his suit jacket and slid it across the conference table to Elizabeth – "a bonus to recognize the quality of your firm's work. Your final billing will be paid as originally agreed."

"Thank you, Mr. Buckminster, Mr. Kennedy. I will see that all the operatives involved share accordingly." Elizabeth placed the envelope in the briefcase that Michael had brought for her.

As they had closed the meeting, Elizabeth had taken Michael Zenner aside to apprise him of their weekend move to Century City and asked him to start putting things into boxes when he returned to the Burbank office. There hadn't been time before the meeting. She had then announced the move to a very pleased Delta Blue management.

James Kennedy nodded as though arranging something in his mind. "There is another case on the horizon which may require your firm's talents once again, Ms Vaughn. I am waiting for the assessment by Jack Strine, our Chief Financial Officer, whom you met very briefly back at the beginning of the current situation. I kept him away from this case to insure you had complete freedom to go wherever you felt you needed to go.

"Once Jack has the elements in line, then we may once again call on your firm to help clean up another of our" -- he paused, his jaw tight -- "our global *messes*." Frowning, he pursed his lips, his pudgy cheeks becoming pink. "Please excuse my coarse comment." He took a breath. "But all that is not why I asked to see you in private. This has nothing to do with Delta Blue."

Kennedy's crooked smile flashed for a moment, then vanished. "I should ask first if you have a few minutes in your schedule." When Elizabeth nodded, he continued. "My daughter, Melissa, graduated summa cum laude at Harvard about two years ago. She is one sharp young woman with amazing potential." He frowned. "But" – he grimaced –"she has chosen instead to bury herself in do-gooding with … with only *feel-good* payoffs." His sneer was quick and gone. "Anyway, Melissa is now executive director of a three year old non-profit devoted to helping parolees and former criminals find a new place in society. Laudable, of course, trying to change these losers into tax-paying citizens … she's even just received a modest $75,000 grant from the State of California, which is only natural. The state is in such lousy financial condition, they need all the tax-payers they can find." Kennedy stood up. "May I pour you some coffee, Ms Vaughn? My temper is getting the best of me."

She nodded. "I'll bring my cup over."

As they stood at the window looking out at the expensive landscape sprawled out below them, all of it once the 176 acre ranch of cowboy star, Tom Mix, Kennedy poured for both of them. Elizabeth noted three Aston-Martins driving one behind the other, two bright red, one green, along Avenue of the Stars. Over half a million dollars of 150 mph toy cars dead stop, choked in traffic.

They turned back to the table.

"Melissa is no loose-minded do-gooder, Ms Vaughn, don't get me wrong. According to documents I have seen, which" – he grimaced – "Melissa is not aware that I know, someone appears to be steadily bleeding her operation of cash. It needs to be stopped as quickly as possible, since if the losses go public, she will never see another donation from any source, even from the state. She can't call in the police as that would go public overnight." He slowly shook his head. " Melissa needs help … but has adamantly refused to ask me for it.

"Do you have room in your schedule to provide that help? Your firm would be paid at your regular rate. I will pay all billings out of my own pocket."

Elizabeth tapped her fingers on the table. "Does Melissa know of your plan to bring in a PI firm?"

"No," he said, his pale face flushed a light pink, "I have not discussed this plan with her, at all. I would trust your judgment, should you take this case, as to what approach I should take."

Noting his reaction, she tapped her fingers again. "What is the real problem, Mr. Kennedy? It doesn't seem to be just the cash."

Kennedy's short laugh and half-smile had no joy. "My God, Ms Vaughn, do you read minds as well?" He clenched his jaw as he slammed his hand against the table. "She has fallen in love with one of the parolees! A two-bit car thief from Germany no less -- damn it all! A two- bit jerk … a …"

Elizabeth raised her hand. "I understand, Mr. Kennedy. Let me determine my resource situation once our move is completed. I will call you on Wednesday afternoon, if that is acceptable."

James Kennedy lowered his head for a moment, took a deep breath, then looked up. "I will owe you, Elizabeth Vaughn, beyond money, if you can help my daughter."

4

Moana frowned. "Bishop Museum wants $300 to copy the Emory manuscript, Boss. " She raised an eyebrow, waiting. It was going to be different with a PI firm operating out of the office. Moana had a dozen questions for the Boss when they had some time.

An unpublished manuscript, *Traditional History of Maraes in the Society Islands,* by Kenneth P. Emory, 1932, was a valuable … no … *potentially* a valuable resource held on a shelf in the Bishop Museum archives in Honolulu. Mackaye nodded. "Let's do it, Moana. Emory did some good work back then with his various articles in the *Polynesian Society Journal*; though why this manuscript of 279 pages was never published is a mystery. Even if it only points a direction toward better material, the savings in time alone could be worth the money." He smiled. "How soon can they ship?"

"They will e-mail it within a couple of days – unless you want it photocopied and mailed which would be cheaper, $150 plus handling."

"Let's do e-mail, Moana, and you get first shot. You are certainly welcome to spend whatever time with it you want. It was your recall of Emory's marae work after all. But," he paused, nodding, turning back to his computer, to return to the world of murder in Hong Kong in 1902, a short mystery story with the working title of "The Dream of a Hermit", " but it should be a good read in any case."

Moana grinned as she reached for the ringing phone on Steele's desk. Her grin vanished as soon as she heard the voice of the caller. She held the phone to Mackaye. "LAPD, Boss. Lieutenant Harper of Homicide … one more time." She shook her head as she walked, danced as Mackaye often thought, out of his office. Polynesian gracefulness was in a class all its own.

"So, Miles, what gives?" He tapped in a couple of words to complete a sentence, then leaned back.

***

Moana looked up as Elizabeth Vaughn pushed the glass door open. She enjoyed the PI's quick warm smile.

"Moana, as your future close neighbor, may I ask a favor?" said Elizabeth as she slid onto the red cushioned chair next to Moana's precisely organized desk.

"Absolutely, Beth." She grinned, "When do you start moving in?"

"Tonight, if it doesn't screw up anything for you here. Then finish over the weekend and have our grand opening – to which you and Steele are invited – on Monday."

"What do you need?"

"I don't have my computer with me. It's on its way back to Burbank. I need to look at the finances of an NPO. Here is the name." She slid a small yellow square of paper across the desk. Hope Beyond Bars.

Moana turned to her computer screen. "How much detail?"

"Their most recent IRS 990 and balance sheet for starters. Names, all the names that come up. I need to know their cash balance and their working capital. Also, did they check Section 6 for diversions."

Moana rotated the screen back toward her as she starting playing the computer keys. "Need a print-out? Diversions? That's NPO-speak for embezzlement isn't it?"

Elizabeth was impressed. How did Moana know about 990's? She grinned. "You are so right."

"I'll have the print-out by the time you get back with your coffee."

***

"Worst killing I've ever seen, Steele. Jesus, I had to work to keep from tossing my breakfast." Harper's tenor voice shook slightly, uncharacteristically. "The most savage …"

"What is it, and how can I help?"

"A young Tarot reader, a Sister Cynthia, was found destroyed at about 10:30 this morning by an elderly client who passed out, and then she was found half an hour later by another client who called 911. This psychic shit turns my gut, but there's a scene here I don't get and I know you know all this psychic crap. I read that novel of yours a year back, whatever it was called, about psychic killers in London in 1890 or something. So, how soon can you get over here? Detective Toni Rodriguez is running the crime scene.

"I have to get back for a bureaucratic to-do downtown. Psychic readers don't rate high on our urgency list, so Rodriguez will be running the show unless something unusual shows up. She hates psychics even more than I do."

His novel had been *Menetekel Masters.* Mackaye had used his own experience as a Tarot reader in his college days as background for the novel. "Where? I'll leave immediately."

***

Moana looked up at Mackaye's sudden appearance.

"A killing. Harper needs some insight. I'll be back in a couple of hours. Cancel lunch for me, Moana." He turned as Elizabeth reappeared, carrying a coffee cup. "How'd it go, Elizabeth?"

She smiled. "Went very well, Steele. Even received a bonus with a promise of another case on the horizon. My move to Century City also went over *very well*. And I have, possibly, another close-in case that Moana is helping me on … if that is part of our agreement."

"It is, and I have a killing to attend to." He started for the glass door. "When do you move in?"

"Start tonight."

"Good. Moana will alert building security so you can come and go without any nonsense." The door closed behind him.

As Elizabeth put the cup on a coaster on Moana's desk, took the print-outs offered, and settled into the red chair, she glanced at the closing glass door. She asked, "Killing? As in human, or financial?"

"The Boss only moves that fast if there is blood involved."

5

Homicide Detective Toni Rodriguez, 24, five and a half feet tall, brown-eyed with short black hair, wore a carefully tailored dark green pant-suit with starched white blouse and a badge hanging from her jacket pocket. Stylish, in a cop sort of way -- her outfit didn't reveal the Glock 23 with its high-count magazine in the holster in the small of her back. Female curves, if you kept them, were designed to conceal guns, among other things. Rodriguez had worked to keep her curves even after her son, Alex, was born three years ago.

A cop was all Toni had ever wanted to be. Her two brothers had become priests -- but she had left the church behind when her favorite priest had been nailed for screwing a little boy. She couldn't look at a bible without thinking of that sobbing little boy, so she never looked at bibles, and her brothers had stopped trying to "bring her back into the fold".

Toni used her maiden name because she didn't want her husband and their three-year old son to be easily tied to her. Her name was not on any property deeds and the family assets were held in a trust, out of reach, in case she was sued for false arrest. And she always took a different way home in case some street jerk tried to follow her, as one media type actually did, to his everlasting education.

Looking out the one window in the reader's sanctum, Toni noted a man down below walking across 7th street wearing a white smock. He was with some kind of cleaning service for the condos in the neighborhood. She had to smile. One time, when she was still a uniform, they couldn't find enough white smocks for a hospital stakeout, so one officer borrowed one from a nearby butcher shop with blood all over the front. Did the job, but sure scared the hell out of some hospital visitors.

Toni turned back to the crime scene for a moment before walking back into the reception area. Blood was splattered on the table, the floor and the psychic reader's chair. The woman, a psychic reader who called herself Sister

Cynthia, had been savagely beaten to death. Toni's stomach had surged when she first saw the room before the body had been removed. She had seen Harper's reaction, even after over fifteen years on the force. Toni knew the guys, the uniforms and the techs, were all watching her reaction, maybe even betting on it, like she had never seen pieces of brain on the wall before, but this was over the top in brutality in her experience.

But ... given the savagery of the attack, why wasn't there even more blood? A few small chunks of brain tissue on the wall, and on a white and gold corner bookcase. Detective Rodriguez had one just like it, from Walmart's, but painted black.

Her first case since making detective -- and they were all waiting for her to blow it. Not that other detectives in LAPD Homicide hadn't blown cases lately, but they were men comfortably ensconced in the organization and the union.

The organization was uneasy. If they didn't jump on her if she screwed up, then it was political correctness run amuck, as the media would headline. If they did jump on her too quick, safely tenured academic feminists and such would be shouting the same thing on some news program or talk show. None of the over-educated critics would waste time learning what was actually going on down in the street. So far as Rodriguez was concerned the academic bastards and bitches should just shut their mouths and let real people get their job done.

Psychic shit Toni could live without. Her mother had become lost in the occult to the constant sorrow of her father and brothers. Even having two priests as sons couldn't move her away from dealing Tarot cards over and over again, letting gaudy colored pieces of cardboard guide ever more of her life. Sarah Rodriguez had died with a Tarot deck clutched in her hand because some reader had told her that a specially blessed deck of the Tarot would hold off the cancer, the vibrations would be right, and all that stupid bullshit -- all for a $50 fee -- for a $6 deck of cards. Toni had priced it in Selana's Ψchic Shop in Glendale. Well, one less psychic -- but the wrong way.

Just the wrong way.

She would nail the ass of whoever had dehumanized this woman, Tarot cards or not. Toni looked back into the violated sanctum. God, there are so many kinds of madness out here.

And now her boss had sent that strange … whatever, Steele Mackaye, to "consult" with her, to support her investigation. Should be here in about 20-30 minutes according to Lt. Harper.

6

Steele Mackaye's stomach tightened when he saw Sister Cynthia's blood splattered sanctum. The coppery smell of drying blood still clung to the walls and furniture. Reddish-brown blotches of all sizes were over the white carpet beneath the reader's gold and white French provincial table. A sculpted mahogany stand in the shape of an open hand that could be used to hold a crystal ball lay on the floor under the window. Long almost-dry drip marks ran erratically across the desk down to the floor. The white-on-white carpet on which the table stood had the signs of the Zodiac woven in an archaic Greek style in an oblate circle. The biggest blotch was on Virgo, his own birth-sign.

Mackaye swallowed hard, his jaw clinched, and turned toward Rodriguez who jerked her head back toward the waiting room.

They sat on the white couch in the waiting room. Claude Lorrain's most famous mystical landscape painting from 1664, *The Enchanted Castle*, or P*sychic Outside the Castle of Cupid,* as Lorrain himself had called it, hung above them in an antique gilt frame. Remnants of black and gray fingerprinting powders were over the five chairs in the room and the coffee table in front of them. Some fluorescent remnants were on door knobs.

"Lt. Harper wanted you to see what we are working with, Mr. Mackaye," said Rodriguez. "So, tell me, Mr. Mackaye, everything you think I should know -- then I'll tell you what I want to know." Rodriguez's voice was low, flat without apparent capacity for joy. Her intense brown eyes were direct.

But she did get the second syllable right.

. "I've never heard of Sister Cynthia. There are hundreds of psychic readers in the LA area. By the way, was she Asian or white? This is on the edge of an Asian neighborhood, but I don't want to make assumptions."

"White."

Mackaye took a deep breath, his thoughts running to his own psychic reading experiences back in his freshman days at UC Berkeley. Odd. Why was Cynthia here, at least 5-6 blocks from a district of more affluent women up near Wilshire? Women were usually 80-90% of any reader's clientele, based on his own experience. Or was it just the rent was cheap and she was new? Had she worked anywhere else? A former client, then … *screw it* … too soon to speculate.

Psychic reading was first about trust, a trust that would be hard to come by if your race didn't fit the hood. "How long had she been in business here?"

"So far as we know now, about two months. Yeah, and she doesn't really fit the neighborhood, so why here?"

Rodriguez waved a uniformed officer away who had appeared at the door who wanted to speak with her. "Later," she said without looking at him.

Mackaye caught the veiled expression of scorn as the cop turned back to the door. Harper said Rodriguez had a solid run as Sergeant operating out of the Rampart Area, but this was the West Bureau, the Wilshire Area.

"You know she was found with a card, a bloody Ten of Swords in her hand? It was obviously put there by the killer for some reason."

Mackaye shook his head. "No. I didn't know that. The Ten of Swords is usually thought of as a bottom Tarot card, and that things can only go up from there. I can't guess what the ten might mean in this situation. How was she killed? Was anything found?"

"With a crystal ball smashed into her skull several times." She reached into the evidence box. "This paperback book. Eden Gray, *The Tarot Revealed*, was found in the drawer of the table in there," said the detective, showing Mackaye the book sealed in an evidence packet. "It's covered with the victim's prints."

"That is one of the classic introductions to the subject of the Tarot", said Mackaye, "along with two or three other works on the subjects."

"It's all marked up with her notes. Still learning it seems." Toni's mother had had a similar book by her bedside. She had kept it lying on top of a bible, which had deeply bothered her brothers.

"It would be of value," mused Mackaye, "to understand if Cynthia was an open-eyed, or close-eyed reader. Not critical, but of value."

"A what?" Rodriguez stopped writing in her notebook and looked up.

"There are two types of psychic readers, Detective Rodriguez," said Mackaye. "Open-eyed and closed-eyed. The closed-eyed are those who genuinely believe that they have psychic abilities or powers … the Gift. That expression dates back to about 1867. They read the cards, the crystals, or palms, then interpret what they believe the power is telling them in the signs for the seeker, the querent, the client.

"On the other hand, the open-eyed readers are fakes. They present psychic reading as an occult illusion. They know the jargon, the history … possibly even better than the close-eyed … but they read the people, not the cards. The Tarot, crystals and such are just props they use to set up the reading, to create the mood of the reading, to set the process of the reading. Seekers expect to see such props and need to experience the process as a kind of reassurance, so the open-eyed readers provide the atmosphere as part of setting up the connection, the final illusion. In either case, the reader, to be successful, must be a very close student of human nature. Just how … never mine."

"You've done readings? Lt. Harper told me that you had some kind of connection with this occult crap," she asked, glancing back at a uniform who had appeared in the waiting room. She raised her hand to hold him.

Mackaye leaned back into the couch. Yes, and he had also had a Claude painting in his little room as well, *Apollo with the Muses*, cost $10 with a busted gilt frame from the Goodwill store. "Yes, back when I was a freshman in college. I once walked through a psychic fair out of curiosity one day and discovered this line of women waiting to talk with an elderly woman who had some wild looking cards spread out on her card-table. I didn't know then what the cards were, but the women were each paying $25, cash, for a twenty minute reading. Like any student, I was always short of money, so I bought a deck of Tarot cards, read Eden Gray's book, and went into business. Over several weeks, I began to learn how to read people. I became frighteningly good, if I do say so." He smiled at Rodriguez's tightly controlled face. She didn't respond. "I began to think that I was close-eyed, that I had the Gift, the real thing. That is, until I met a professional mentalist at a local magic shop. He was going to give a lecture on performing mentalism that night which I later attended. I laid my psychic successes on him with, I admit, some childish enthusiasm." Mackaye laughed softly. That memory hadn't jumped up in years. "The mentalist listened politely, then suggested that with my next client I tell her the exact *opposite* of what I would have normally told her, and study what happens."

"The opposite? What would that prove?" Her face relaxed some. Rodriguez was curious, and Mackaye's weathered face was actually friendly, he spoke quietly, no macho put-downs.

Mackaye raised a hand. "I'll explain in a moment. I thought the mentalist was nuts, but he was a top act, making more money than I could even dream of. So, when I re-opened my little shop a couple of days later, I had been making almost $120 a day, cash, by the way, so I definitely didn't want to shake things up too much. But I did what he suggested. To my shock, all of the four clients that day were as impressed with my *wrong* reading as they had been earlier with my *right* reading. They all said I was right on and happily paid my fee, telling me how much better they felt about their directions and their upcoming decisions. At the end of the day, I had banked about $80, closed up shop … and never did another reading.

"What the mentalist had wanted me to see and experience was that it was the client's need to hear and see what they needed; it had nothing to do with the Tarot … or really with me. Whatever they heard as part of my spiel that fitted with what they needed, they kept, and ignored all the rest. They basically convinced themselves. Psychologists call it subjective validation."

"Conned themselves? Sounds … crazy." Rodriguez cocked her head. Her mother had conned herself? Her face paled momentarily, then recovered.

Seeing impatience in the stance of the uniform at the door, he said, "Let me quickly finish. About a month later at that same magic shop, I met a man who was introduced to me as a successful open-eyed reader … from New Zealand actually. When I told him of my learning experience, he laughed. He said that he had encountered that back at the beginning of his career, which was when he also realized that he was really only a rented friend, someone on whom his clients could unload anything, knowing that he would never criticize or ridicule them, or betray them; but just listen to them and help convince them that what they already wanted to do was the right way to go. The psychic props provided a trusted process, and he had no medical degrees on the wall that could suggest that their being there was because of a mental health problem."

Mackaye laughed. "Sorry for the prolonged biography, Detective. Anyone making a living in sales has to know how to read people. Policemen and politicians included."

"So, you can read me?" Rodriguez challenged. "Never mind." She glanced at the uniform and tossed her hand to acknowledge him.

Mackaye smiled. The detective clearly thought she was reading him. Not likely.

"Twenty-five bucks for twenty minutes of Tarot bullshit?" Rodriguez's voice rose. "Better than a dollar a minute. So why do all psychic readers I've ever seen live in the low rent district? That's eighty dollars an hour, Mackaye; better than … $150K a year, all cash, with almost no overhead, with most of it stashed away from the IRS. Better than most people in LA can ever hope to make. She reads that book, and, to give her some credit, I'll assume maybe a couple of the others, then sets up her place here, puts out purple handbills -- we found a box of them in the closet in there -- and starts telling people how to live their lives. Christ," Rodriguez snarled, "a damn con that should have been wiped out a hundred years ago! Probably was taken out by someone who didn't like what Cynthia had been doing to their life." She reached into the evidence box and withdrew a purple handbill, giving it to him.

Mackaye began to scan the purple announcement.

"Be back in a minute, Mackaye." Toni Rodriguez stepped away to converse with the uniform. She nodded and turned back as the officer left the room and resumed her position on the couch.

Even purple, the graphic layout was subdued, devoid of the usual pentagrams and other familiar New Age symbolism; more like a doctor's almost prim announcement of opening a neighborhood clinic. Sister Cynthia would provide intuitive counseling, the more current label for psychic reading … but the hours … readers' hours often ran to as late as eleven at night, but Cynthia's were from 7:30 am to 3 pm. She was targeting working women in her marketing area. The women who came to her would not go to her competitors who did not open, generally, until ten or eleven in the morning … of which there had to be several somewhere close-by. Cynthia may be new, but she clearly understood the business. Her pricing: $15 for fifteen minutes using the Tarot as an aid for their confidential visit, no appointment necessary before 9:30. She was really targeting the local market, not the upper class near Wilshire. $20 for fifteen minutes for appointments after 9:30am. She must have walked the neighborhood, checking on competition and pricing accordingly, and evaluated the financial status of her potential clients. Cynthia had done her marketing homework. Impressive. Mackaye wished he had had the opportunity to have actually known her.

"It appears," said Steele Mackaye, returning the handbill as Rodriguez resumed her place on the couch, "that Cynthia wanted a practice, a sanctum that would more resemble a doctor's office, without the usual quirky New Age trappings, to give it a more professional and comfortable feel. Sister Cynthia put at least a couple of thousand dollars of furniture in there. I suspect that all of her earnings were going to pay off her furniture."

Rodriguez paused to look at him. She said, "Tell me what you see." The detective pulled out her iPhone, pressed a button and handed it to him.

At the first photo, Mackaye pursed his lips and shook his head. The psychic reader's body lay across her table, her head a grotesque mass of blonde hair and greyish-red pulp, her white dress or robe soaked in red.

"Oh, Hell!" he whispered. He held the photo for a moment, pausing to collect his thoughts before looking at the next photo. Sister Cynthia's body had been removed revealing the face-up Tarot cards spread roughly across the desk like a … 76 card game of stud poker. Two cards were missing. One card was set aside from the rest, or had been pushed aside when she had fallen forward onto the desk. It was the King of Pentacles.

Then Rodriguez handed him the bloody Ten of Swords.

"Morgan-Greer," Mackaye said.

"What?"

Mackaye turned the card over. A couple of odd marks in blue marker on the black background among several blood smears. "I've suggested the usual relevance of the Ten of Swords, but …" He pursed his lips. "I don't see anything … except that the killer spread the cards, Cynthia didn't."

"Since Cynthia was still reading Gray, she most likely used the Ancient Celtic method of divination, or possibly the Tree of Life spread. Neither method of spreading the cards would look like this. So, Detective, have you checked the cards for fingerprints since they were obviously last handled by the killer?"

Rodriguez frowned. "No, but we will. What else?"

Mackaye dropped the bloody Ten of Swords back on the coffee table and took up the iPhone still showing the desk with cards spread across it. "The killer was likely a man with black hair and dark eyes," he said softly.

"What! Don't try to con me, Mackaye!"

"Detective, this card, the King of Pentacles, here on one side of the image," he said. "Either it was pushed there when Cynthia fell across the desk and therefore means nothing; or Cynthia had pulled it out of the deck to use it as the Significator card in the Celtic spread. In which case, it represents the inquirer, the visitor, a man with black hair and dark eyes. The Significator is used in the spread to represent the person, the client. If it had been a woman with black hair and dark eyes the card would have been the Queen of Pentacles."

"What about, say, a blonde blue-eyed man?"

"That would be the king of Wands."

"What else?"

"May mean nothing," said Mackaye, "since, again, the card could just have been pushed accidentally into that position, but, the card is reversed, upside-down toward the client. That can mean that the man is making perverse use of his greatest talents, whatever they may be."

"Richmond," Rodriguez ordered the uniformed officer standing guard at the door. "Get two others and question everyone in this building and anyone in the building next door about seeing a black-haired man with dark eyes coming into this building between 9 to 10 this morning."

She turned back to Mackaye. "We know about when she was killed since she was alive for a reading at 8:30 and her next client came for an appointment at about 10:30 and found her … like that photo. The client was an elderly woman who passed out and was discovered by another client who called 911 just before noon time." She shut down the iPhone and slid it back into her jacket pocket. "Let's hope for the Celtics, Mackaye." Rodriguez stood up.

"And what else did you find?"

"Haven't found anything that says where she lived, or what her real name is. She put a phony home address on the office lease and paid three months cash up front, probably so her landlord wouldn't dig any deeper."

He looked around the waiting room. "There's nothing more here."

Rodriguez turned as a uniformed cop knocked at the door. "Yes?"

The officer consulted his notebook. "Black-haired man, heavy set, with dark eyes was seen coming into this building at about nine-twenty AM. He held the entrance door for a female tenant who lives next floor up in this building. She was carrying in some packages. Gray goatee, black mustache, tall, very well dressed. Unforgettable, she said. Like meeting Count Dracula himself."

7

"Why can't you work with your hands, like an honest man?"

Marku's father had cursed him, again and again, emphasized with hard punches to his shoulders which would often leave Marku's arms hanging limp and numb. His father had still ripped the money out of his hands that Marku had earned by smuggling a few cartons of Camel cigarettes into the country from Yugoslavia.

His father and brothers had been typical honest farmers in the west of Romania who had adulterated their grain shipments to the government and then paid off the government purchasing agent -- like every other Romanian.

Cat e spaga? -- How much is the bribe? -- was the Romanian national slogan equivalent to *e pluribus unum.*

When Marku Antonescu finally ran off the farm for the final time shouting "*Du-te dracu!* -- go to hell! at his raging father who shook a pitchfork at him, Marku vowed never to respect anyone but himself. All the rest were just shit -- except those who have the money-eye.

***

Antonescu smiled as he walked briskly down Western Street four blocks away from the sanctum of Sister Cynthia, the *curvă,* the blonde whore. He had dropped his briefcase, wiped clean, into an open dumpster. A postman would lose his invisibility carrying an alligator-skin briefcase. Any *idióta,* idiot, could pull a trigger, that required no toughness or talent. He preferred to use his hands so that the mark would know who was taking their life.

Once he had finished destroying the little whore he went into a stair well and changed to become invisible. He had folded the Armani suit and tie along with the stage whiskers into the brief case. It took only two minutes to put on the U. S. Postal Service uniform he had been carrying. He took out the large padded white Priority envelope filled with newspapers he would carry as a prop, then closed the brief case. The case, with his working tools for this assignment, would go into the dumpster in the alley behind the building.

He had tainted the Armani with the DNA from at least eight other men to screen any of his that might adhere to the cloth. Marku laughed. So, let the *caralieu*, the police, play their clever forensic games they are so proud of. He spit the word. Their *cãcar,* shit, computers would not bring them closer to him.

Antonescu had learned very early that you became invisible to everyone as soon as you put on a uniform -- particularly that of postal workers who always have an accepted reason to be anywhere at any time. No ninja could be more invisible than a postman. There were other invisible trades but a postal worker had always worked best, anywhere in the world.

Anywhere.

Maybe his father had been right, Marku laughed. Honest work *was* done with the hands.

8

Elise Markel's small broad body was compressed into a set of green sweats. Long blonde hair hung limply down her back. "Never saw him before. But he was frightening." Her lips tightened. "Really ... really scary."

"How?" asked Mackaye. "In what way? Did he make a move on you or physically threaten?"

She shook her head, looked at Detective Rodriguez, then back up to Mackaye. "You with the police, too?" she asked. Markel had flinched when Rodriguez had shown her badge. Now Markel stood with her arms held tightly across her chest, her back pressed against the edge of the doorframe.

"No," Mackaye replied. "You were saying ..."

"Okay if I answer, Detective?" Markel asked. "I don't want any trouble with the cops."

Rodriguez nodded. "Go ahead. I want to know the same thing." She edged closer in with Mackaye looking over her shoulder.

Markel turned back toward Mackaye. "He was just ... just creepy. Too smooth. Too polished. Had the most beautiful empty, empty smile -- like he was just exercising his face. Too much in command, like everything was going to be his way, no matter what. He was going to open that door whether I wanted him to or not. I was raised in Bavaria around men who always acted in charge of everything. That's why I'm over here now." She sniffed, then wiped her nose with a handkerchief she had been holding in her hand.

"Did he have any accent?" Mackaye asked.

"Did he kill that woman, that, that psychic?" Elise Markel had turned pale. "Cop told me." Her apartment was one floor above Sister Cynthia's sanctum. "Never saw her -- but psychics only bring trouble, just trouble. Wished she had never moved in." She shuddered. "Nothing good happens when a psychic is around."

"We don't know if the man you saw had anything to do with the death downstairs, Ms. Markel," said Rodriguez, gently.

"He seemed to have an accent, definitely not Bavarian ... but I couldn't recognize it. He didn't say that much. Maybe Eastern Europe but I don't know. Maybe not so much an accent -- just the way he spoke the words, the rhythm.... I don't know anything else. Are we finished?" She edged backward into her apartment.

"For now," Rodriguez said, moving a step back.

After the door closed, Mackaye turned on the detective. "That woman was scared stiff. You better have some uniforms visible around here for a day or two, or she's going to run before you can put her with one of your forensic artists."

"Mackaye, damnit! I know scared when I see it. I'll have a police artist up here within an hour -- and there will be a cop on this floor in five minutes."

"Good. I want to see that picture when it's done ... if you agree. Someone with that breed of presence has to leave some kind of trail. *Anyone* ... anyone who can project menace like that is either a hell of an actor -- or a merciless killer who enjoys his work ... or maybe both. Something more than just psychic readings is in play here. Whatever the hell it is." He started to turn toward the stairway. Then, "One thing, Detective ... did the crystal ball have dust on it?"

Rodriguez's jaw dropped. Another shot off the wall. Harper had warned her that Mackaye would have a different point of view. "I don't know. Why would that matter?"

"It would strongly suggest whether Cynthia was killed twice, as I suspect now she was, which would, naturally, be confirmed with an autopsy."

The detective stared at him for a moment, then punched her speed dial. "Nettles, did the murder weapon, the glass ball, have dust on it along with the blood?" She listened for a moment, then another. "Okay, thanks." She turned to Mackaye. "Yes, there was dust still on the crystal ball, so now explain."

"First, Detective Rodriguez, I am not competing with you. I am not a detective. You are in charge. I am just a wandering consultant with some odd experiences that Lt. Harper has found useful in the past. And I am Steele, by the way," he said extending his hand. "Let's start over."

Toni flashed a quick smile. "Toni," she said.

"Cynthia seems to be new to the game. She probably had the crystal ball sitting on that hand-like mahogany stand for display, not in actual use."

"She was still reading the instruction book, then?"

Mackaye grinned. "Exactly." He wanted to sum up, there was work to do. "The classic book on the proper handling of a crystal ball is by Theodore Besterman, about 1965 or so, which teaches that the crystal is always covered by a white silk scarf unless it is actually being used. The presence of dust says that there was no scarf. A scarf would have been covered with blood, but there is no evidence of one. The dust proves that. Crystal gazing as a general topic is called Scrying in the trade, by the way." He tossed his hand. "Just an aside."

She nodded and wrote in her notebook. "The second killer …?"

Mackaye nodded. "If Cynthia saw the first killer go to the window to pick up the dusty crystal, which would have been easily available, then she would have run and her body found somewhere else, but there she was draped neatly over her expensive table. Very likely the first killer who was probably seated across from her as she prepared the Tarot spread, just stood, reached across the table and snapped her neck; then he walked out. The second killer comes in, finds her dead, and maybe in frustration, since he likes his job, smashes her skull into oblivion with the crystal to prove to his employers that he was there." He turned to go. "I'll do some digging to try to locate where Cynthia lived and get back to you with any feedback I can get, hopefully later this afternoon. It's clear that Cynthia either saw or knows something critical that two groups wanted to silence her. So, we've got to move. There may be more blood ahead."

"Agreed, Steele … and thanks," as she watched him drop down the steps two at a time. She flipped her cell open.

. He had Moana on his cell when he reached the first landing. Morgan-Greer was the key. A special edition deck with a black background with multiple white stars instead of the usual blue background … where had Cynthia found such a deck? Then he called The Erdnase Café out in Tarzana in the Valley, a coffee-pastry shop with an exceptional magic shop and library in the back. No one except those well known to Johnny "Bat" Masterson, the owner, would ever get past the door to the back.

The Café was decorated with drawings, aquatints and old photographs of early casinos, notorious gamblers, and memorable saloons. The tables were all covered with green baize like a saloon card table, with three racks of books along the walls relating to gambling and its gaudy history, including, naturally, several copies of the 1902 bible of gambling with cards, *The Expert at the Card Table* by E.S. Erdnase, a pen name. No one knows with any certainty who Erdnase really was. The book itself has never been out of print.

The magic emporium in back was decorated with rare conjuring posters from Bat Masterson's impressive personal collection, including a very rare poster of Anna Eva Fay, the woman Harry Houdini had once called, "… the greatest female mystifier".

***

Toni confirmed. No man matching Elise Markel's description of Dracula had been seen leaving the building, bloody or not.

\

9

Elizabeth Vaughn smiled and sipped the unbelievable coffee. "Steele, can I serve this coffee to my clients when they visit? They have suffered enough on my PI coffee in Burbank."

"Absolutely. You could increase your hourly rate as a result."

Elizabeth laughed softly, then placed her cup on a small circle of deep brown Hawaiian koa wood that rested on the small table beside her. "Presentation went well. There will even be a bonus paid beyond the billable hours, which is always nice. But I have a problem."

Mackaye held his warm mug in his hand, waited and was silent.

"The CEO of the firm took me aside to ask if I would take on a project for him personally. It relates to his daughter and the non-profit of which she has become executive director. It appears the NPO is bleeding cash. He wants me to find out where the money is going because, and I have not confirmed any of this, there is no entry in Section 6 of their form 990, a lot of the money seems to be going out the back door."

"Not an uncommon situation for an NPO, I understand, but I am certainly no expert."

"Because his daughter is involved, the CEO is leaving it to me as to how I interface with her: either as a PI with my time paid by her father, which apparently would cause her to erupt or explode in some way; or as something else with my PI interest hidden. I haven't committed to taking the case until I work out my role and do some background checks on some of the people involved in the NPO, which is called Hope Beyond Bars, by the way. You will likely start hearing that name if I move ahead."

"Focused on doing good things for ex-cons and such?"

"Right. But who am I?" She frowned. "I need a valid reason to ask embarrassing questions. I need to be a creditable outsider," said Elizabeth.

Mackaye got up, walked across the office to straighten an island painting that had shifted off-center. Must have been another 3.5 tremor. There was a fault line running down Santa Monica Boulevard that could move sometime, with the potential, according to geologists, of a maximum power of a 7.0 quake. He turned back. "How about being a screenwriter for a planned documentary on saving ex-cons? Get some overnight business cards made up, and ask away. Nothing opens people up, I've found, than the prospect of being in front of a camera."

Elizabeth nodded, her head cocked. "Perfect. You've done that yourself, it seems."

Laughing, Mackaye dropped back into his chair. "Ah, the PI as mind reader again. Yes, but that is a story that can wait."

"What about backup? They might want to call my producer?"

He picked up his phone and hit a speed dial.

"Eric, Steele Mackaye."

The voce from the speakerphone on Mackaye's desk was deep, resonant and cheerful. Laughing, the voice said, "Steele, man, where have you been? Still dodging around those dead places in Polynesia? Though with that Polynesian goddess you have there, I couldn't imagine doing anything else. And, yes, my Ten Commandments documentary is going well, thank you for asking."

Elizabeth grinned. She liked this 'Eric' already. "Ten Commandments?" she said.

"Eric Mendelsson, let me introduce Elizabeth Vaughn, who has just moved her PI firm from the wastelands of Burbank into our offices here in Century City. She has a case where I think you could be of serious help."

"Ms Vaughn, my pleasure. And let's talk the Ten Commandments when your time is not so short, and far more valuable than mine."

"To oe faearaa, Mr. Mendelsson."

"My God, Moana has gotten to you already, Ms Vaughn ... and it is Eric."

"There is a great deal behind those marvelous eyes," she said. "A great deal. And I am Elizabeth."

"So, Steele, how is it I get surrounded only by near-sighted overweight screenwriters, and you get goddesses?"

"Clearly divine intervention, Eric." At which they filled the room with laughter.

After a moment, Elizabeth said, "In a new case, Eric, I need to pass as a screenwriter" – she nodded to Mackaye, who raised his cup in acknowledgement – "for a documentary on convict rehabilitation. I am investigating some strange financial events at an unnamed NPO. I might need you to confirm my assignment, to give me legitimacy. And thanks for listening."

There was a moment of silence, then, "Can do. Actually, Elizabeth, I did a doc on ex-cons back maybe 6-7 years ago, which bombed with distributors. They said the film was too pessimistic, you know, the revolving door thing, no great success stories, and so on. And it *was* pessimistic. Hell, it couldn't be anything else. What's different about your gig … if I may ask? I know you have confidentiality concerns.

"And, for the record, everyone, I am on the team. I will also make sure that my Number Two knows you are doing preliminary work for us, Elizabeth, so you will be covered. I trust the man across the desk from you for any number of unmentionable reasons."

"Actually, Eric, I don't know just yet where the bodies lie. I will be making my first call and visit early next week. My firm will be moving into our new offices here over the weekend and should be up and running by the end of Monday. I can alert you to when I make the first contact, which may generate a confirmation call from the NPO." She hesitated. There was something else … damnit, what was it? The ah moment hit. "Eric, you need to know what I look like in case you are called."

"Yeah, you're right. Steele, give me Elizabeth in living color. I need to see her through a man's eyes. I suspect she would be too modest."

After Mackaye's two sentence description, at which Elizabeth blushed, Eric said, "Haunting blue eyes. Yeah, as I said, surrounded by goddesses.

"Elizabeth, sounds doable. Steele has my private number which he should give to you. Steele, come around soon. I've been known to serve a beer or two even while carving stone tablets. That invite includes you as well, Elizabeth, whenever your time permits."

Moana opened the door. "Excuse me, Boss. Bat is on the phone. He just walked in the Erdnase door from The City."

10

Elizabeth had followed Moana out the door talking about business cards. Eric had hung up with Steele's promise of a visit soon.

"Bat, how did The City work out?" Mackaye leaned back in his chair. Johnny 'Bat' Masterson was reliable, knowledgeable on all aspects of the conjuring arts … but, he could turn very edgy if he thought he was being pushed into a corner.

Bat Masterson's voice was a resonant tenor, honed on numerous secondary parts in various television productions. His ability to project "disciplined nastiness" as his resume declared, was his major selling point; that, and a marked resemblance to a young Errol Flynn, but Bat preferred the company of young men to Flynn's notorious harems.

"Could work up to a sustaining role, Steele. I would be a minor hero with growth potential as my agent assures me. What gives? The guys said you had called earlier."

"Morgan-Greer. Have you sold any special edition black Morgan-Greer decks in the last two or three months, or so?"

A short pause, then, "What's with Morgan-Greer? I don't run a psychic shop, but I always have some Rider-Waite Tarot on the shelf in back. But wait, wait … yes, the last batch of various decks of cards from U.S. Playing Cards about 10 maybe 12 weeks ago, just before I did a spot on a new show in development, I remember.

"I have U.S.P. doing a couple of custom decks for me, for the Café, along with refilling my stock of the standards. Been a run on the usual trick decks, Brainwaves with special backs, Svengali's with large indices, some oddball strippers, and, my God, even some Bee-backed Mene-tekels, along with a bunch of really weird new decks for the discerning magician who can do the latest card flourishes. The local U.S.P. sales guy sold me about ten Rider-Waite Tarots left over from somebody's order that got reduced at the last minute, and threw in a couple of black Morgan-Greer's he happened to have for good measure."

"Do you still have the Morgan-Greer's?" asked Steele.

"No, sold both decks. Was surprised, they went quick. Maybe order a case for next time."

"Do you have a record of who bought them and/or where you sent them?"

Bat's voice took on an edge. "Hey, man, this is getting a little weird now. What's up?"

"Bat, I need to locate a woman who may have bought one of those decks. It is urgent." Moana's calls to the various New Age and psychic shops in LA had drawn mostly a blank for black Morgan-Greer in stock. Three decks had been sold but to areas outside of LA. Images on M-G were too challenging to relate to, was the usual shop answer, Moana had explained. Queered the vibes, they said.

"Give me a minute. I'll have Angelo check out back. I know they didn't go over the counter. My on-line and mail-order side is now almost as big as my in-house sales."

Steele sipped the last of his coffee and brought "The Dream of a Hermit" back up on the screen. He had to get three key characters from Hong Kong out to Lamma Island, about 30 minutes sailing southwest of Hong Kong into the South China Sea. But the plot just wouldn't bend ...

"Yeah", said Bat, coming back on, "got addresses on both sales. Apparently the local psychic shops aren't carrying Morgan-Greer as much as they used to. Got a pencil?"

Two women, Hilda Fox, and Christina Montgomery-Smith. Fox was three months ago, and the other was about two months. A moment to write down the addresses. No phones or e-mails. Both women had called in their orders.

"Bat, many thanks. This could allow a major move. Once the confidentiality condition is removed, I'll explain everything, and buy you a drink of your choice."

"So long as it's not at my place," he laughed. "Wherever, it will be Macallan 18-year. So, Steele, when can I book you for another lecture? Had some good vibes from your last one on Polynesian magic. Opened all kinds of eyes to different slants on presenting mentalism ... including mine. And," Bat added, "bring that island goddess of yours. Moana is in a class by herself. And you can tell her I said that. When she comes, all the drinks are on me." Bat paused. "And for your information, Steele, Stephen Minch is coming down from Seattle next week. Should draw a large crowd. He will be speaking on tricks performed with Crowley's Book of Thoth deck. For entertainment purposes only, of course. But Stephen told me that he would be available, sort of off-site, to discuss other dimensions of the deck with a suitable audience. See you then?"

"Thanks Bat. Yes on Stephen's lecture. Anything he says on the conjuring and related arts is worth careful listening. I have Crowley's deck on my shelf next to Stephen's *Book of Forgotten Secrets*.

"I'll give you some dates to choose from for my lecture when I know them myself. And I will pass on your invitation to Moana." He smiled as he ended the call. Would be a lot of fun, and Moana would enjoy the off-site discussion with her insights into Polynesian techniques of divination.

But reality swiftly swept away the momentary feeling of fun. Mackaye mused as he walked to his window. So is … was Cynthia either Hilda or Christina? Heavy haze was moving in, starting to obscure the mountains as the sun began to touch their peaks. Could be dangerous driving tonight along the coast.

Or was Sister Cynthia someone else entirely?

He dialed Toni Rodriguez's number, but hesitated
before hitting Send. Who *was* Sister Cynthia? She was more
intriguing than any plot he was working on. She was clearly
intelligent and … something of an entrepreneur. Mackaye
canceled the call and started for the door. He should be the
one to do the initial digging. Toni had other areas to dig in he
couldn't touch. If the doors stayed closed when he knocked,
then he would call up the police artillery. Christina was the
closest, about 40 minutes down the 405 in Mar Vista on
Walgrove Street, not all that far from the coast.

11

Magic has but one dogma, namely, that the seen is the measure of the unseen.

As Mackaye took the Venice Boulevard off-ramp from the 405, it occurred to him that Somerset Maugham's observation from his 1908 novel, *The Magician,* could apply to police work as well. The haze continued to thicken as he merged onto Venice Boulevard into unusually light traffic. His 1988 Mercedes 560SL moved quietly, effortlessly up the speedometer. The lack of traffic would cut about ten minutes off the drive. He should arrive just after five.

Bronze, with black leather interior, large rectangular European headlights, he had been stopped a number of times

by drivers and others, even other 560 drivers, wanting to
know what kind of a car it was. The European lights
transformed the front end of his 560 into what the German
designers had originally intended, not the anemic four-eyed
American version. Though the 560 had been designed for a
maximum of 150 mph as an 'Autobahn Roadster', Mackaye
had never gone above 95; but it was obvious even then, that
there was a lot of muscle still on call, only a short flex of his
foot away.

Any time he was in Venice brought up odd memories
from a happily misspent youth of fire pits on the beach with
amazing girls, the surf boards stuck upright forming a
windbreak wall behind them, guitars, ukuleles, flutes, songs
with ever more outrageous lyrics as the pizza, more beer than
was wise, occasionally some equally unwise highs with
whatever began to hit home. Hell, it had been plain fun …
almost half a century ago.

The tall narrow two-story white house took his breath
away. Mackaye had not known such an extraordinary, stark
modernistic house would exist in what was a middle class
neighborhood of houses about 25-30 years old. Up three
concrete steps, he pushed the paneled wooden gate open. The
opaque white fence surrounding the property stood about six

feet high. Nothing but a simple bolt held the gate closed. The yard was small, bright green, precisely manicured with heavy flowering bushes all around the base of the fence. The impression of carefully spent wealth did not match with a psychic reader practice, real or fake. Yeah, that and the $780,000 the present owners paid for the house three months ago – in cash. But the new owners were not named Montgomery-Smith, but rather Reber; from Hawai'i according to Moana's quick data search.

Mackaye closed the gate behind him and took a step toward the front door, then stopped. Some lights on the second floor went on, then one, and then two went off, shadows moved across the tall narrow windows of the second floor. Shadows without curtains. Looking up he caught a glimpse of motion on the flat roof, probably a party of some kind up there. A chill spread across the lawn. Mackaye tried to smile. A psychic chill? Or just the sea breezes picking up. Now he smiled. The plot for "The Dream of a Hermit" was still churning in the back of his mind. There *was* a way to get his three characters to Lamma Island.

He moved on.

"Yes?" The doorbell had been silent, but the door was opened within only a few seconds. Dark-haired with some sun streaks, she was middle-aged, attractive with brilliant green eyes along with a healthy tan dressed in white gym sweats and sweater, a white sweat-band around her head. Her quick smile had a coquettish slant to it. "You are not the pizza man… are you."

Mackaye grinned. "An incisive observation. I'm Sam Milliron, a writer of non-fiction works … without a single movie deal." He handed her his business card.

Laughing, she said, "Step in, Mr. Milliron, we have something in common already. I'm Jade Reber." Scanning his card, she raised an eyebrow. "That Century City address looks awfully rich for a … writer/historian."

"I get paid protection money to keep from attacking certain professors," he grinned. "The address also intimidates publishers. But not movie producers, it seems."

The first floor was stark in its minimalist stainless steel furniture with a flamboyant Picasso lithograph, along with a few small framed photos hung seemingly at random. There were noises from upstairs.

"Did you live in Hawai'i long?" said Mackaye. "My present project that has brought me to your door is the Tarot."

Jade Reber frowned. "Here, for Tarot? Why?" She hesitated, unsure. "How do you know about Hawai'i?"

"Tourists collect clichés, but former residents collect special memories, like that small photo of a road on Kaua'i there in the corner, the red frame. There is a magnificent white house near the end of that road. To the right, as I recall."

Her mouth dropped open. "How …?

"I have traveled Kaua'i and recognize the road, and I can smell the Kaua'i coffee brewing, the peaberries. That's an element in a coffee blend I use at my office." Mackaye continued. "There have been only two decks of special edition Morgan-Greer style Tarot decks sold in the last three months in Los Angeles. I would like to know why. I am examining different styles of Tarot as part of looking at the need of people, both religious and non-religious, to seek family advice from total strangers whose only qualification seems to be fluency in paranormal gibberish.

"Someone named Christina Montgomery-Smith purchased one of those Morgan-
Greer decks and gave this address where she wanted it shipped. Thus I am here."

"Let's go ask Christy why. The stairs are there in the corner. We were just starting to go up to the roof waiting for the pizza man. So, they get the Tarot man instead. Follow me, Sam."

Jade Reber moved smoothly across the mirror polished floor and started up the spiral wooden stairs with Mackaye three steps behind. Every corner of the house was lighted. Hardly a shadow anywhere, except those windows. After a few steps with the noises above getting louder, Jade stopped. "You said paranormal gibberish, Sam. Is the paranormal real or fake? I hope fake."

Looking up into her suddenly troubled green eyes, he said, "In my experience it is fake …even, at times, brutally fake."

She nodded and continued up the winding stairs.

Reaching the top, Jade Reber clapped her hands for attention. Two teen-age boys wearing LA Dodgers t-shirts were pushing each other around, two adults, a young woman in black and pink sweats, a bald middle-aged man in shorts and tennis shirt with a towel around his neck sat at a long narrow black table All stopped to look at Jade. There were footsteps above on the roof.

"This is Sam Milliron who is not the pizza man, but is here to talk with Christy. Where is she, Mark?"

The tennis player pointed toward a door. "In the library, Honey. And welcome, Mr. Milliron." A delicate tone pulsed three times. He pointed at the two boys. "Get the pizza, men, we are starving." The boys scrambled around the adults to disappear down the stairs. "And bring it upstairs," he called after them.

"Come, Sam, I'll introduce you to Christy. She is our daughter, by the way."

***

Sitting at a small metal table, Christina Montgomery-Smith looked up from the Tarot spread. Tree of Life, Mackaye noted, noting as well that she was obviously not Sister Cynthia. He needed to get moving. Hilda Fox was now their only known option.

"Christy, this is Sam Milliron, who is interested in that deck of Tarot you have." Jade Reber left the room.

"My deck of Tarot? Why?" Dressed casually in a sleeveless blue and white sweater and washed jeans, she was probably late twenties, recently had a wedding ring on her finger, wore glasses, with her blonde hair short.

"If I may, Ms Montgomery-Smith?" said Mackaye, holding the back of chair at the table.

She nodded, studying him as he sat at the table. "Do you know the Tarot?"

"I know a Tree of Life spread when I see one. Is that your most trustworthy spread?"

Her half-smile was not friendly. "You mean does it tell the future?"

He shook his head. "No, I meant does the spread consistently satisfy your meditation needs. The Tarot, as I have come to understand it, is not always for telling the future, but more for clearing your mind, for allowing your whole being to empathize, to fathom actually, the concerns and needs you are facing." He had used that pitch with some success three or four decades in the past.

Time to get moving, not to interfere.

Christy sat silently, her brown eyes fastened on Mackaye. "You sound much like my mentor. I apologize for being so cold. Please" – she beckoned – "move in closer. How may I help your project?"

"Why Morgan-Greer as opposed to, say, Rider-Waite? Have you been long with the Tarot?"

"Two years I wasted until I met my mentor last year. He took one look at my Rider-Waite and threw them out his window, saying I had been wasting my time on such children's rubbish. I was absolutely shocked. I didn't like Rider-Waite, but I didn't think I had an option. He gave me his deck of black Morgan-Greer and things began to open before me. Simple as that." Christina grinned. "I finally bought my own deck a couple of months ago. He had allowed me to use his deck for almost six months, then said I was safe to solo with my own deck. Black back only, of course." She smiled. "He used to fly planes for the Navy, many years ago. He turned to the Tarot to understand where he was in the civilian world when he went off active duty."

"The Tarot ended your marriage," said Mackaye. It was time to leave. Jade's concern about the paranormal was family-based. That was obvious, but he was not there to "fix things" as one psychologist in a neighboring office in the tower had once described his practice.

"Yes. My husband hated my mentor and the Tarot. I finally walked out two months ago."

Mackaye stood, sliding his chair back into place. "Thank you for allowing me to intrude, Ms Montgomery-Smith. I have what I need."

***

At the bottom of the stairs, Jade asked, "What is happening with Christy? Can I get her --back? I know. You're a total stranger and I ask something like that. I must need help myself."

"No, Jade, you're a mother who cares," said Mackaye. "Just keep caring and listening. Christy does the Tarot because the cards seem to listen. Once she is confident that you will listen, without criticism, her need for the cards and her mentor will begin to fade. Your husband also has to listen. And don't allow the boys to ridicule the cards like her former husband obviously did. Just love her unconditionally … and give her time."

"How long?"

"I'm not the psychologist, Ms Reber. A psychic reader, a fake whom I greatly respect, once told me that his job was that of a rented friend. He was the one person his clients could come to, dump everything on his table, and know with certainty that they would be received with respect. You need to be Christy's most reliable friend," he smiled, "rent free."

**

The 560 started immediately. Toni would meet him at the home of Hilda Fox on Arlington Street. She was about twenty minutes closer and would wait for him. Mackaye punched off the Blue Tooth™ connection on the steering wheel, moved the polished solid burlwood gearshift to D … he pressed his foot down gently.

The fog was finally, firmly in place, hovering, as if looking over his shoulder.

12

Elizabeth Vaughn slashed the end of the roll of tape on the box of books and pressed the tape down flat. Her husband, Jim, in his favorite Red Sox sweatshirt, was laughing with Charlie Wang in a corner as they dismantled a bookcase. Charlie would be first joining the firm Monday at their new address. A lanky Taiwanese who spoke both Mandarin and Cantonese backed with serious military justice experience, and now with an American passport, Charlie would be put to work first thing Monday morning on, potentially, a major long term client involvement. Gregory Hood Importers, Inc., were headquartered on the central waterfront off 3rd Street in San Francisco, with offices in LA and Honolulu, along with their first retail store scheduled to open in San Francisco in a month which would specialize in jade and gold.

She had liked Greg Hood on first meeting him at the
San Francisco airport, he leaving and she arriving, a tall
ruggedly featured man, grey hair, sharp inquiring blue eyes
with a wicked rakish smile, and decidedly unmarried. And,
happily, with many potential PI problems.

Michael Zenner folded down the flaps of a box
holding a printer. He glanced at his watch. 6:40. "Dinner time
anyone?"

Jim stood up, stretched his back. Tall, dark brown
hair, cut short, a solid 200 pounds, with dark designer
stubble… and a quick grin. "I'm buying. The finest gourmet
Neapolitan pizza this side of Positano. Preferences anyone, or
my judgment?"

Tiny Angelica Wallace looked around a doorway.
"Your money, Jim, your call. I'm for Peroni though, if they
have it." She disappeared.

Elizabeth took a deep breath. Her first office, with her
own firm, her first dream had come true. The walls were bare
now. Now it was going to be different in Century City.
Moana had been busy responding to a call from Steele when
she had pushed through the glass door. Moana mentioned

some kind of a Tarot problem, then went back to her computer screen.

It was going to be different, but – she grinned – it was going to be great, by God. "I'm in for Peroni, too."

But then Jim already knew that.

***

"If Fox is not here, I'll need a warrant to get in, Steele," said Detective Rodriguez, officially. "By the way, forensics is going crazy over the stuff found in the dumpster behind Wriston's building. The fake whiskers say that the briefcase and its contents were the killer's, but the suit, Armani, tests out to have been worn by about eight men. No way to pull out the killer's DNA. We are dealing with a serious pro, Mackaye."

Mackaye nodded. "Understood. We will still nail him." He gestured toward the door. "If she's dead, she can't file a complaint," he said.

"I'll call Lt. Harper." She turned away.

Mackaye bent down to the lock. Nothing complex, he heard its click within a few seconds. The apartment building was an old stucco building with some renovation, but still reeked of the glorious '70's.

"He says okay, Steele, but we have to watch our step … very closely. If it is Fox, he needs to get a warrant in place asap."

Mackaye pushed the door open.

The room was neat, but barren. Fox had rented the apartment furnished. Nothing, as he and Toni scanned the living room, suggested anything about who lived there. Except maybe that bookcase next to the aged couch. About two shelves of books and papers. And …

"I'll take the bedroom, Steele", she said.

The large dust covered black Bible was copyrighted 1936. It had been inscribed to Hilda from Aunt Louise, 1998, with the direction never to let dust accumulate on it. But it wasn't the Bible itself, a King James version, but the neat assortment of clippings, notes and letters each secured by large paper clips kept inside the cover. When Mackaye lifted the Bible out to place it on the small circular dining table, he found a manila file beneath. Dropping the Bible on the table, he went back to the file. On top was a copy of the lease agreement for the psychic reading office … he had found Sister Cynthia.

"Toni, we have found Sister Cynthia!" he called.

Beneath the lease were pro-forma cash flows for the next two years, tracing Hilda's, or Cynthia's hopes for her psychic practice. Noting her assumptions, the good, the bad, and the extrasensory, the projected cash flows reflected a practical understanding of the real world. Cynthia was not a dreamy mystic who felt some spiritual call, but a practical entrepreneurial businesswoman trying to … Mackaye hesitated. Trying to what? What was she coming *from* that a psychic practice became … became the best way, at least for two years? There were notes from her surveillance of the neighborhood. Locations, hours, fees, and the various selling pitches of her seven potential competitors. He recalled that Cynthia had listed Spanish on her handbill as a language option, has had four of her competitors. The three others, in addition to English, spoke Korean, Chinese and French, respectively.

Clearly she had done her marketing homework, done it carefully. And clearly, Cynthia was an open-eyed reader.

Toni was suddenly by his side. "The lease for her reading sanctum, Toni. We now have a firm identification. Perhaps your people could start … wait a minute. She also used the name Cynthia Wriston, see here on this postcard. Why not track both names in our search, see where that might lead."

She was on her cell phone immediately. Mackaye was on his to Moana, then began to sift through the rest of the file. Letters from someone named Pierce Mahoney. He skimmed one, then two, three and finally four. Mahoney was laying out how to set up a psychic reader practice … but the letter dated the earliest, about six months ago, was an acceptance of Cynthia's apology for something that had happened between them in Tijuana. What was that?

He called Bat Masterson. Clearly, Mahoney was a mentalist.

"Yeah, Steele, what's up?"

"Pierce Mahoney. Who is he? Is he any good?"

"First Morgan-Greer, and now Mahoney? Connected?"

"Might be."

"Mahoney is a top mentalist on the East Coast, based, I think, in New Jersey. He was out here testing the waters I guess about six, maybe seven months ago. Part of his shtick is to have a new beautiful woman as a partner almost every season. much like the Bob Brown and Brenda act of years ago. Remember them? That is a tough, tough way to do it, but Mahoney has been doing well."

"Saw him twice on my recent 'survey' trip to San Diego maybe … six, eight months ago. My trip was crap, but I caught Thoughts in Parallel, Mahoney's act, at an exclusive Tijuana club, invitation only, $300 dinners for two sort of place. They were damn good … almost real. Really had me guessing, and more than once. The woman was a small attractive blonde, but never got her name clearly, but she was solid, handling the crowd, even shifted to Spanish when necessary, even telling jokes in Spanish, for God's sake! Just solid. She was gone when I went backstage to invite them up to the Erdnase to meet some agents and maybe lecture. Something must have happened that night between them. Mahoney was really, really steaming. That's it."

"Would Cynthia Wriston mean anything?"

A point of silence, then, "Damn, Steele, that was her name. Saw it on something in the dressing room. Just couldn't pull it up before. Wriston, yeah, that was it."

"Thanks, Bat. That solves a mystery or two. Will explain when I can." As he closed his cell, he looked at Toni.

"I have forensics people on their way, Steele. Lt. Harper has been notified and is getting a warrant in place, and I am going to have to keep all that stuff on the table. And, officially, thanks. The woman had no record and no fingerprints on file. So, my options were getting limited for understanding who she was …" She raised her hand, turning back to her humming iPhone. "No question? Okay." Toni grinned. "Steele, another homerun. Wriston *was* murdered twice. Snapped neck and then destruction of her brain a little over an hour later. You saw that because of *dust* on a crystal ball? I must be reading the wrong books."

Mackaye laughed. He started slowly skimming through the Bible materials and the file. The first news clipping was from upstate New York. What was going on?

13

Marku Antonescu was dressed invisibly, even for after seven with the house lights coming on along Arlington Street. All evidence of his earlier appearance was gone. The man with the money eye wanted some problems solved: $30K for one and $50K for the other. Cash into the right account within 6 hours after completion. There was $10K up-front in place. No one tried pushing him more than once. Tonight, identify, track, then set up the *ciocan,* the hammer. He was relaxed, Marku smiled, he was always relaxed. He always tossed any of his airplane books he read when traveling if the killers in them were not relaxed. That meant the author was only writing fantasy, and he didn't need fantasy.

It had taken him almost three weeks of searching to find the place of the blonde *psihic*, the psychic, but they had found her home in a day. How? She had had so many names, so many faces. He would have killed her just for the trouble she was causing him. He laughed briefly. But only if some one with the money eye had needed it.

Marku Antonescu relaxed, comfortably invisible. He frowned. Who had smashed her head in when she was already neatly dead, and he had made sure the King of Pentacles was left on the table, properly positioned. He knew someone had picked up on the card. He had been 'delivering mail' while he watched the police scrambling everywhere.

He started to smile, but saw two women approaching with filled grocery bags. They were talking, laughing, confiding secrets then one suddenly looked over and met his eyes directly. Marku looked away instantly, but too late. The woman was startled.

Beneath the blanket, Marku gathered his legs, ready to leap up if necessary.

***

"Okay, let's call it a night," said Elizabeth. "We can pick things up tomorrow at, say nine? We can make the first run to Century City about then. Not too early, it's been a long day." She turned. "And thanks, Charlie, for digging in before you even walk in the door."

Charlie Wang grinned and nodded.

"Jim and I will have the van tomorrow. Security at the tower is ready for us. Moana said she may be in to work on a project. You all will really like her. She is a knockout," said Elizabeth, noting Jim's crooked smile which widened when he caught his wife's inquiring look.

***

Mackaye stood at the window in the darkened bedroom lit only by streetlights coming on. The forensics squad was finished in here and was working in the living-dining room. He had left the Bible materials for them to examine. Just skimming the materials from the Bible, it was apparent that Hilda Fox thought only of herself as Wriston, not as Fox any more, except for that New York clipping, but there hadn't been time to read in full. But she seemed to have earlier professions, earlier names that caused an odd question to come to mind. Of the various names and professions, astronomer, Egyptologist, even a jewel thief it appeared … given all that, just which one of the many personae of Hilda

Fox was actually the target of the killer? She had been killed twice. Were they killing two different people?

Looking back out the window, Mackaye frowned as he scanned the street, the traffic beginning to fade. Homeless people generally don't solicit after the sun goes down, too threatening one of his research sources for a novel-in-progress had explained. Too risky, could easily bring the cops, and draw too much attention. And they never set up housekeeping for the night on the street side of a sidewalk.

Two women walking carrying bags had caught his attention when they had abruptly stepped away as they passed the homeless man stretched out, wrapped in a blanket, his back up against the traffic sign support. There were two full white plastic bags lying next to him. He hadn't made any move toward them that he could see, so what was the issue …?

New to the neighborhood, perhaps. Yeah … along with a whiff of his engaging odor.

Mackaye turned back to Toni.

"Forensics has the fingerprints off the clippings and stuff, Steele. I scanned most of them on my iPhone. They should be showing up on your phone in a minute or so. Let me know what you think, I've got to get going. Place is going to have yellow-tape across the door for the next 2-3 days."

Mackaye acknowledged Toni's wave with his own, noted the download in-progress on his phone, and, one last glance out the window, started back toward the living room.

Toni was gone, one uniform was on the door, the techs were closing up their cases.

Oh, shit! Mackaye started to run.

14

"The Mahdi ceases to be the Mahdi

the moment he admits

he must stop at any moment."

About eight months ago, Steele Mackaye had helped an instructor at USC with his early research on a thriller novel about General Charles 'Chinese' Gordon set in Khartoum in 1884 at the time of the rise of the Mahdi (the Rightly Guided One) revolution. The comment of Tewfik, the former Khedive of Egypt, about the Mahdi in the May 20, 1884, issue of the *Pall Mall Gazette* (page 10) in London had also triggered a short story of his own.

The moment you stop being unique in the eyes of the people, they will desert you, or as the Khedive had so emphatically suggested, they will assassinate you … in anger … in disappointment … but most likely for betrayal of their dream.

Mackaye dropped down the stairs two at a time, his knees twinging. He couldn't wait for the elevator to come back up three floors.

The Khedive was certainly right.

***

Detective Rodriquez nodded to the salute of the patrolman at the entrance to Hilda Fox's apartment building. She had never seen him before, but he clearly knew who she was. She caught Lawrence on his name tag, memorized his face and walked out. Mackaye had proven his value as a "wandering consultant". But now the clippings, notes, letters and the Fox bible itself were under her arm. She would draw a late night tonight. Then compare with Mackaye's reading tomorrow morning. She had had only time to scan a little over half of the material. A double killing of a single individual – Toni had never heard of one, but with her luck, she had caught the first one on her watch.

Some dark clouds were bringing night a little faster than usual, she noted as she walked to her car. The homeless man, a sandwich-board man with his gaudy shirt advertising a restaurant, was gathering the assets of his life together as she passed. A couple of white plastic bags seemed to hold most of it. Even with his head partially bowed, she couldn't mistake his angry face. Probably picked the wrong corner to

...

She kept walking. At her car, Toni opened the passenger side, started to drop the bible and materials on the seat, then stopped. Something didn't ring true. There were no homeless shelters within six, maybe seven blocks. When she had started at Rampart, her senior partner had told her to know the shelters, because nobody remembers seeing a homeless person unless they are out of place.

Toni glanced back.

***

Marku watched $50,000 walking toward him. His face twisted with *fierbe,* seething, furious. Catching the eyes of that woman with the bag, that could have caused *probleme prost*, stupid trouble, not useful trouble. He knew he was approaching the edge of his invisibility as the sky darkened.

He should be moving away toward anywhere, just anywhere. At this point, Marku had intended only to identify the two targets …but here she comes … the cop at the door had his eyes on her and now on him as well. He bent to gather the plastic bags filled with wadded up newspapers, to fuss, mumbling to himself, pulling things to him, the custom Taser with its lethal ultra-high voltages dropped down into his hand. But if he attacked and had to run, he would run away from his invisibility, abandon his *invizibilitate*. Almost a perfect setup, but … Marku thumbed the safety off the Taser.

Shock, immobilize, the knife, then …

***

Mackaye jumped down from three steps up and ran to the entrance, lowering his shoulder to blast the door open, only catching sight of the cop at the last moment, slowed, pushed the door hard, to run down the stairs to the sidewalk, leaving the cop staggering against a railing, cursing him. Toni was near her car. The homeless man with the phony white bags was on his feet, turning toward her, starting toward her in a slumping awkward walk, the kind of walk you would learn in acting school.

"Toni!" he shouted. "Toni!" Mackaye ran hard toward the lumbering man, only a few feet …his knees exploded in pain. His left knee suddenly gave way. He fell across the sidewalk, slamming his head up against a tree. Stunned, he couldn't move.

Toni turned back at her name, saw Steele fall into the tree trunk, to the homeless man only three or four feet away. A chilling wave swept down her back when she connected with his eyes. Pure brutal menace!

Both of them -- *but get one*. Marku fired the two charged projectiles from his custom-built Taser as the *politest căţea*, the bitch cop turned toward him, his finishing knife slipped smoothly into his left hand. He couldn't curse. — the words stuck in his throat as the stun darts slammed into the bible under her arm. He threw the Taser at her and ran hard toward the narrow pathway that paralleled the side of the next building. That was his emergency escape route that he had paced out earlier, set it up, then paced again, before morphing into homeless.

Marku heard the man shouting behind him, but it was the Glock he glimpsed coming into the hand of the căţea that spurred him on, he ran as though his hated father was behind him with a pitchfork. In a moment he was into the pathway, five steps more -- he would be invisible again.

Toni heard Mackaye coming up slowly behind her, as she dropped the bible and swept her Glock 23 into her hand. She thumbed off the safety, as her attacker disappeared around a tall hedge.

She stopped at the corner of the hedge, then palming the butt of her Glock she crouched down, stepped out, quickly sweeping the muzzle of the gun back and forth, then up each side. The homeless guy with the Taser had vanished! Toni stamped her foot, then walked rapidly, examining both sides. Her cell at her ear as she walked, Toni ordered all remaining personnel to the pathway and to the other side of the building. He had to come out somewhere.

"Behind you, Toni," said Mackaye, limping as rapidly as he could. Damnable 63 year-old knees.

"The fucker vanished, Steele. Just sitting there watching our circus, then tries to make me with a Taser – a damned Taser!"

Breathing hard, Mackaye managed, "Didn't want any noise. He planned to finish you with a knife in his left hand.

But damn, I should have recognized those phony plastic bags, and he was in the wrong place, and …" He threw up his hands. "I was so blind I can't believe it." The pain was slowly fading from his knees, but he still had to walk carefully. Christ, he couldn't run after killers more than once a week any more. Mackaye took another deep breath, then slowed his wind in-take.

Toni was back on her phone. Five uniforms around the building, including one coming toward her on the pathway. Lawrence from the front door was coming around the hedge. "Anything, anything at all?" she asked into her phone.

From her frown, Mackaye knew the answer. He started slowly down the edge of the pathway looking for a footprint. Homeless didn't fly out of here. And retrieve that Taser he threw at Toni. Might prove interesting.

"Here!" shouted Mackaye. A partial footprint. He pushed the hedges apart to reveal an abandoned coal chute, its door hanging open from one hinge. He couldn't fit, but the young cop running up could.

Toni nodded. "Looks black down there. Garcia, keep your light handy, and shout good and loud if there's any trouble." She turned. "Lawrence, be ready to back him up."

Without hesitation, Garcia dropped his peaked cap, freed his billy and flashlight, positioned himself, and disappeared down into the black chute. They heard him hit the concrete floor. A moment, then, "Detective, nothing down here! Some footprints toward the other side of the building. I'm following."

Toni pointed toward the chute. Lawrence immediately dropped down the chute. She was on her phone as Mackaye walked back to the street to recover the Taser, then to return to the other side … no, too obvious. This man was a pro. He wouldn't drop down that chute unless there was an almost immediate route out. The footsteps were faked earlier, probably. Did Homeless think of everything?

With the Taser in his hand, Mackaye took a needed deep breath. Police in the basement and on the other side. Toni running the show. He would head back down the pathway and look at the other side, the side away from the building.

Walking more rapidly, the wide beam from his backup LED flashlight running along the pathway, and under the branches of the hedges to the left, away from the adjacent building. Nothing. Maybe he was giving Homeless too much credit. A few feet more, still no indication

of ...

There!

Mackaye knelt down; moving the beam slowly up and down, There was a deep gouge in the smooth dirt. He pushed his way into the tall hedge which easily bent apart.

Ah, crap!

The black six-foot ladder was braced against the brick wall that backed the hedge. The first rung was almost pushed down into the soft dirt. Homeless had hit the ladder hard, climbing up to the top of the wall and over. Mackaye was on the phone with Toni, whose choice of words was more imaginative than his.

He jammed the Taser into a coat pocket, his cell into another, and started to climb. Toni's urgent, "Be careful!" ringing in his ears.

Homeless' Plan B had been solid. Maybe, as Mackaye threw his still throbbing left leg over the top of the brick wall, potentially as deadly as his Plan A.

15

Toni was fuming. "He faked us out like we were all amateurs!" She was standing near Mackaye at the white wrought-iron gate to the half-empty parking lot on the other side of the brick wall.

"Homeless faked me as well, Toni, probably easier. And we still have the issue of just which of the two killers he is: the first who snapped her neck; or the second who bashed in her skull. Just how we will separate that out I have no idea."

Toni grimaced, then said coldly: "Whichever, we'll nail the bastard and then ask him, not very politely.

"I'll run the Taser for prints, Steele, and then break down its construction. That may help. It's not US made, that is clear. I'll check the FBI if they have a file on foreign-made

Tasers. And I have two squads doing door-to-door. Damn, Steele, he was waiting there for us. Waiting!" She looked up at him. "And a belated thanks for warning me. I might have been an easy target … if not for that bible and you." She shrugged, then grinned. "I owe you lunch with a gourmet beer."

"That's a go. I'll get started with the copies of the Bible materials you scanned," said Mackaye, "see what might be there. Reconnect in the morning? Your call."

"Yeah, that will give me some time to look at the stuff as well."

"Nine-thirty, my place? Moana will have brunch ready. Better than cop coffee and local cardboard doughnuts. And you can meet my new PI tenants."

Laughing, Toni started to turn to a uniform calling her. "You got it, Steele. See you then. And, thanks."

***

"Sharks Roaming in Venice Canals" was in the lower right hand corner of the first page of *The Argonaut,* a local weekly paper for the Marina area. As Mackaye walked comfortably, his knees back to normal, toward the elevator to his condo, he read: Five young leopard sharks each about three feet long were observed gliding near the surface of Sherwood Canal. No danger, but sharks of any kind had not been seen in the Canals for a number of years. How these five had penetrated to the Venice Canals from the Pacific was uncertain.

Homeless was an uncertain roaming shark by any definition, but lethal.

***

Punching some buttons and pouring some spring water got the coffee going, from a pound of pure Blue Mountain Jamaica, a gift from an editor wanting another Polynesian book; a few chunks of cheese and prosciutto for a late supper, and then onto the Bible materials.

Hilda Fox was clearly an intelligent, but deeply troubled woman. Based on a clipping from the Lake Placid *News* in upstate New York, about eight years ago, a man from Saranac Lake was found dead from rat poisoning. Fox had written in blue marker, "Got Him!" on the article. Had she poisoned him, and if so, why? The man ran an auto repair garage. He was known for a violent temper, but he could make "any car in any condition wake up and sing" according to a quote from a neighbor. Mackaye pushed it to one side. A killer? But probably too long ago to be relevant.

Three letters clipped together from Egyptologists at major museums ridiculing her claim to have discovered new information on the female pharaoh, Hatshepsut. One had written "Stop pretending and get a day job!" in red ink. There were angry black slashes across the pages.

A similar group of four letters from different astronomers to her claim of insights into the orbit of an undiscovered moon of Uranus, with emphatic though slightly more polite rejections. On one letter, however, the writer, a professor of astrophysics at Columbia University, had written, "Highly imaginative calculations, with some promise, Ms Fox, accurate so far as you have gone, but why?" There were no angry slashes, but rather evidence of tears blurring the ink of the comment.

The two groups of letters covered a span of almost six years. Mackaye shook his head. Who or what was Hilda Fox? What was she trying to be?

A rubber-banded group of five engraved business cards all white both sides, the embossed image of a prowling big cat of some kind, resembling the figure used by Jaguar as their logo, and the words Le Chat Blanc. No address. The White Cat. A printer's receipt from a New York Chinatown printer, addressed to Cynthia Wriston requesting approval of the samples. Now Hilda Fox had become Wriston. Just who or what Le Chat Blanc was … was answered in the next clipped group of newspaper clippings from the New York papers. Le Chat Blanc was a jewel thief!

Cynthia, as he now thought of her, had written a note in an elegant hand in white ink on black paper, apparently for later framing:

Pablo Picasso, the most brilliant con-man of the twentieth century (after Sigmund Freud) said it. Picasso summed up his tangled life with, "Great artists don't borrow, they steal".

Wriston had double-underlined the two words. She had written in white on the back:

Yes, steal!! Self-confirming success.

Stealing doesn't require the judgment of a professor or academic expert to define success. Cynthia needed affirmation of who she was, that was obvious.

***

Cynthia had apparently stolen a collection of expensive costume jewelry in a "daring, but highly foolish" daylight maneuver at Diamond City on Broadway in NY. The store manager had been quoted laughing, "Why would anyone with brains risk several years up the river for a $400, at retail, pile of German silver jewelry? The woman was nuts."

"Just wait', Cynthia had written along the border.

But then an article, about two weeks after Diamond City, described the audacious theft of a red jade medallion worth over half a million dollars from Edward's, a very exclusive boutique jewelry store on Park Avenue. The story emphasized the extensive security measures at the store. *Clearly the thief must have had inside help,* was the emphatic conclusion of the reporter that Cynthia had underlined and written, "No way!!"

The medallion had been at Edward's for cleaning and some unspecified meticulous repair. It had been in the prominent Xi family of Hong Kong for almost six generations. Sailor Xi, the young woman who was the Director of the Xi Foundation, was furious. The medallion was to be on display for only one day and it was never for sale. How, Sailor Xi demanded, how could the thief had known the exact day if not tipped by one of Edward's 'trusted' employees? Even in ink, Sailor Xi's bitter sarcasm came across in spades.

The new manager at Edward's, Alain McNair, from Boucheron and Tiffany's in Paris, had insisted he had no thieves in his employ, but he had no explanation for how the thief could have known of the medallion. The reporter noted that McNair had brought many of his "eight-figure friends" from Paris when he joined Edward's.

Mackaye added another note, then went to the kitchen for a refill on coffee. He shrugged, stopped to open the small cabinet, Ali Baba's treasure Laura had called it, where he kept his chocolates. He grinned as he chewed slowly. Laura. He missed her supportive presence and so much more. Her cancer had just kept coming back. He shook his head. Chocolate had always been their great stimulant for intelligent thinking and conversation.

So how had Cynthia known of the medallion … unless, if McNair was right, it was just an incredible coincidence? The Xi family was not ready to accept any notion of coincidence. He could imagine Sailor Xi breathing fire.

Mackaye sent an e-mail of questions to a friend who dealt extensively in the Hong Kong financial markets regarding the Xi Foundation, then turned back to the clippings.

My God! Cynthia gave the medallion back! There was a small ad that Cynthia had circled torn from the New York *Times* that asked a certain person to contact him at a number using the name they both knew. A second ad signed by the same man expressed the regard of the mutual friends for the caller's sensitivity.

The next article from the *Times* announced the return of the red jade medallion from someone called Le Chat Blanc. Then Le Chat Blanc disappeared from the file, as though Cynthia had closed her career as a jewel thief.

Toni had had time to only scan a portion of the second file stuffed into the Bible. He would see the rest tomorrow morning. He turned to the Pierce Mahoney letters.

Thoughts in Parallel was engraved in black and silver on the letterhead. A second-sight act starring Pierce Mahoney with his beautiful partner – whose name was blank. Mackaye skimmed the three pages of the letter. It outlined the act, what the partner's responsibilities would be, with some suggestions for her preparation for their rehearsals, and her pay which would start at 20% of the gross. As her contributions to the act grew so would the percentage. If things did not go right, then the percentage would not go down, she would just be "released". There was no e-mail or phone number on the stationary, so it appeared to be a form letter for a prospective partner to read.

Mackaye reached for his cell. "Bat, how can I contact Pierce Mahoney? I thought I had something, but didn't."

The noise in the background was too loud to hear, then the sound of a door pulled shut. "Yeah, Steele. Sorry, the guys are jumping to some unbelievable card routines. What do you need?"

"Pierce Mahoney. Do you have e-mail and/or a phone for him?"

"Yes, but not with me. I'll e-mail it to you later. I have to get back to the paying customers."

Steele leaned back. That was all he had for now. While he now had a modest understanding of who Hilda Fox was, he still had no input to why two killers had to kill her. And who were they killing? An Egyptologist, an astronomer, a jewel thief, or a psychic reader, or maybe even someone else? And was it the same persona, or were the two killers killing two different people?

Sharks were definitely roaming the neighborhood.

16

Moana looked up. Elizabeth had her back against the door, pulling a cart with boxes piled on both shelves. She immediately ran to hold the door open.

"Right on time. Welcome home, Beth. How can I help?"

"Thanks, Moana. The whole crew is behind me with the rest of our first load. Just holding the door and pointing the direction would be very helpful."

"Will do. The coffee and brunch is ready in the conference room, any time."

Elizabeth Vaughn grinned her thanks and pushed the cart.

***

Mackaye dialed Pierce Mahoney's number in New Jersey. First the phone, then an e-mail if …

"Mahoney. What's up?" The voice was firm and insistent. Like "Don't waste my time!"

Mackaye introduced himself then said, "Cynthia Wriston. What can you tell me about her?"

There was a long moment, then, "Cynthia? What has happened now?" His tone was softened but neutral.

"She's been murdered."

"Killed? My God, Mackaye!" Then silence for a moment. "Give it to me, all the details."

***

"Moana, this is Jim, my husband."

Moana extended her hand which Jim Vaughn gripped gently. His Red Sox sweatshirt had become filthy. He smiled. "You run a taut ship here, Moana. The place is beautiful, and I love those red doors." He sipped his coffee. "And this coffee is almost supernatural… reaching for a solid engineering description, of course."

They were all sitting in the conference room, taking a break from delivering the first load, with some preliminary box openings. Beth had already introduced everyone, so everyone was just drinking and enjoying the spread. Charlie Wang had particularly complimented her on the island dishes. "Read about food like this, Moana, but never experienced it before. Just great. When does the next plane leave for Mo'orea?"

**

"Cynthia was … was just exceptional, Mackaye," Mahoney said, his voice gentle. "She answered my ad in *Variety*, asked all the right questions, and we started working, rehearsing. She was ready to go live in four weeks. Four weeks! No woman I have ever worked with, all intelligent as well as beautiful, were ready until almost eight, sometimes even longer. Cynthia was not a strikingly beautiful woman, but there was something there that was just … compelling. She was the dream of anyone doing second sight. If you know Bat, then you have an appreciation for what I've just said."

"I do," said Mackaye. "But what happened?"

"Oh, Christ, I just can't believe she's dead. Give me some time." After a moment, Mahoney continued, "We were booked at an exclusive invitation-only club in Tijuana, had knocked out the audience for the third night in a row. Hell, you could still hear the applause through the dressing room walls, when Cynthia said she had to leave the act, that night, right now.

"I was stunned speechless. I had just raised her percentage to 40%, the highest I had ever gone with a partner. I pull down around $2,000 a night for most gigs, sometimes more, and we could work four to five nights a week. Do the math. You are looking at a serious six-figure income. And Cynthia just put on her coat and walked away. She said she had seen someone in the audience that she had hoped never to see again. Someone who could injure her, as she called it. Then she was gone. She was sobbing when I last saw her.

"I was pissed off as all hell."

"So," said, Mackaye, "where did the psychic reading come from?"

"About two, maybe three weeks later, she sent me a long apology," said Mahoney, slowly. "Even promised to try to pay me back everything I had paid her. That was just ridiculous. Then at the bottom of her letter in a p.s. she said she was looking at opening a reading practice in LA. Could I suggest some books?

"I had gotten over the feeling of betrayal. She had worked hard and helped make the act even better than anything I had been able to do. Killing time in hotel lobbies, we had talked about a reading practice, sort of as an off-season exercise. Cynthia had some unique ideas about staging a setting for a reader. So we started corresponding about psychic readers, the marketing aspect, and so on. She was an open eye, if you know the term. Her questions, as always, were right on. And she understood what I was saying. I suggested Morgan-Greer, particularly the special edition, for her own deck, pointing out that some clients may have other preferences, but absorb one deck thoroughly as her foundation. And so on, you may know the drill yourself."

"Yes," said Mackaye. "I did readings back some time ago when I was a freshman at UC Berkeley, which led me into the magic world which I have been in in some way ever since." He paused. "Did she ever mention a jewel thief, Le Chat Blanc, or the fact that she apparently murdered a man in upstate New York about eight years ago, or about Egyptology, or astronomy?"

"What! What is all that about?" Mahoney said, his voice on edge.

"It is all about Hilda Fox, the woman you knew as Cynthia Wriston. She was a jewel thief, a killer, a second sight partner, and tried to be all the rest. She was a very troubled woman, just how deeply disturbed only a psychiatrist could say. Anything about any of that would be helpful to the police investigation, I am sure,"

"My God. troubled? No way! Cynthia was the most confident and controlled woman I've ever known. Maybe the second sight and the psychic reading were the most satisfying … maybe they were the most successful in meeting whatever psychological needs she had." Mahoney went quiet for a moment, then another. "She did mention Le Chat Blanc, asking that I promise never to say anything, but now?" He took a deep breathe. "Anyway. She had stolen a red jade medallion and gave it back. She was very proud of how she had done that, and it was a coincidence. She was planning to steal something else, but there it was.

"But the Xi family just couldn't accept that and put the pressure on the jewelry store manager, McNair, I think, to find out who the woman was in order to prove to the family that none of his employees had been in on it, which he did.

He hired a tough PI named Harry Pie to track down Cynthia. Somehow, Pie had connected Cynthia with Le Chat Blanc. So the pressure from the Xi family forced McNair to send a thug after her even after she had given the jade back. To cover his own ass, that's obvious. That's it. I know nothing beyond that."

"Pierce, thanks for your help. I owe you next time you are in LA. I'll e-mail my address and e-mails."

"No, Steele, you owe me nothing. I owe anything of value that I've contributed to the memory of the best partner I will ever have." He hung up.

Moana appeared at his door. "Come join us, Boss. Detective Rodriguez is here with the PI group." She watched Mackaye's face. "Something tough, Boss? You don't look good."

Mackaye looked up. He nodded as he stood. "I'll explain later, Moana. Everyone has met everyone?"

"All on first name terms already." She smiled. "Toni, I think, is anxious to get on with your work."

"I really need some of your Mo'orea creations, Moana. Lead the way."

17

Mackaye shook hands around while balancing a plate of Moana's amazing Tahitian shrimp in coconut-vanilla sauce. He had over-dosed on this before, and would any time he could enjoy it. There was at least half of the spread yet that he hadn't even looked at. The shrimp stopped him cold. The depression he had felt with Mahoney's hanging up was starting to fade, but how did that all fit with Cynthia's killings?

He sat next to Charlie Wang, began to trade some Taipei memories, particularly of the glass-encased Guanyin statue which had survived a Japanese bombing without breaking. Toni sat across from them. She slid the manila file of bible materials over, along with a CD.

"The CD was tucked into the bible, but I can't figure out what it is. The Lieutenant couldn't make anything of it either."

He opened the manila file, began to spread things out. "I'll get it on my computer right away. Be right back."

"I know you can't talk, Toni, but all that stuff looks very strange. Is that a Tarot card?" said Charlie. "I know nothing of Tarot and really don't want to, unless naturally, a client needs the knowledge."

"Yes, that is the Ten of Swords from a Morgan-Greer deck. The suits of Tarot, as I have discovered with a quick study, are Swords, Wands, Cups and Pentacles. I don't know that much myself, but I am having to learn."

"May I see it?"

Toni gave the card to Charlie, then forked more of Moana's Polynesian fish salad. Unbelievable flavor.

Charlie grimaced. Ten swords driven into the back of a blonde white guy face down in the sand in a pool of blood. *Zhŭ!* God! But with a horizon in the distance, suggesting, probably, barely, that something better is on the way. He shook his head. You would have to be really up against the wall to look at stuff like this. He turned the bloody card over, odd-shaped white stars on a black background, single-ended, so the Tarot reader could detect a single card in the deck from the back, out of the whole deck. More bloody smears – zhŭ! Could it be?

Her mouth half full, Toni saw Charlie's hard expression. "What?" she managed, swallowing everything at one gulp.

"All right if I scratch a bit here?" He put his fingernail on the edge of a bloody smear.

Toni looked closer. The blue markings that neither Steele nor her could understand. She nodded. "Careful though."

As Charlie chipped delicately at the bloody edge, small bits of dried blood fell away. A moment, then another. Damn, he was right!

He looked at Toni as Mackaye re-entered the conference room. "This," he said, tapping the now fully revealed square with a double line through the middle with one line stopping at the edges of the square and just below the square was another partially concealed more complex character. It was simplified pinyin. There was no mistake. He had seen this signature twice before, once in Taipei and then three months later in Hong Kong. The evidence in both cases had been even more bloody than this Tarot card and the crushed skull of the Tarot reader.

"It is the signature of Xī Yīng, White Falcon," said Charlie. "He is known as the *èmèng*, the nightmare man. Very high-priced, maybe $75-100,000 minimum for a hit … always, always very messy. His style is to dehumanize his targets. He never uses a gun, of any type. Up close and brutal." He shrugged. "Forget him, Toni. He is already out of the country, only God can know where."

Mackaye looked at Toni. "We have one killer nailed, it seems." He turned to Charlie. "Is he part of the Xi family of Hong Kong?"

Charlie twisted to look up at Mackaye behind him. "Ah, the Xi. A very rich, very … very determined family for maybe five-six generations in HK, but, if I hear right, if you are in their circle, they will protect you, however. But no Taiwanese need apply. For some reason, they detest Taiwan. They will trade with Taiwan merchants, but never trust them. My father dealt with the family a few times, then never again. Whatever they negotiate, they pay, but always in dealing with the Taiwanese, pay months late. I don't know why. My father had to deal with them, they were his best customers for a time, but they always stretched his cash flow almost too far.

He dropped them, finally, and had to work hard to replace them."

Toni took her ringing cell to a far corner of the conference room. After a few minutes, she returned to slump down in her chair her face a mask of disgust. "Gone! The bastard is gone! Right through us. We had a surveillance camera shot of him, still homeless, getting into his car, a white Aston-Martin DB9, and driving off. APB out immediately. How can you miss a DB9? The car was stolen. It was just found ten minutes ago with the interior on fire."

"What now?' asked Elizabeth, looking first at Toni, then Mackaye.

"Send in squads to saturate the neighborhood. Somebody must have seen something we can use. Thanks for the marvelous food, Moana; I'll be back for recipes." With a quick wave, Toni was gone.

***

Marku had ditched the homeless costume and burned the car. He was now dressed in a deep blue Zegna suit with a cell to his ear. The money eye wanted a change in the engagement but for more money. He might have smiled, but never show emotion on a job. Never!

***

"Let's go crew," said Elizabeth, putting her plate on a tray. "We have to finish the basic move tonight, then Sunday afternoon and Monday morning we get reconnected with the world and start servicing our clients again.

"Charlie, Greg Hood will be in town late Monday for a first general client meeting here. You need to get some background in place.

"And thank you, Moana, so much. The brunch, as Steele called it, was just beyond description. Leave the plates. We will clean everything up when we get back later tonight."

Charlie Wang was already at the door. "Will do, Elizabeth. Looking forward to it. Heard some real interesting things about the remarkable Mr. Hood."

Mackaye said, "Do you have a minute, Elizabeth? Would you take a look at my computer? With the experience you summarized at Delta Blue you might have an insight that I just don't."

18

Elizabeth Vaughn settled into Mackaye's chair. The screen was a list of names, cities all over the world, and dollar amounts for each. There were comments of some kind, obviously coded, after each name. She scrolled back up to the top. More of the same, but with some kind of descriptive motto or name at the top... again coded. Along with a date. About six weeks ago. She scrolled down to the bottom. 89 names and locations.

Elizabeth went to the door. "Angelica, Michael, can you come in here please?" She looked back at Mackaye's quizzical expression. "I've seen something like this before, but Angelica and Michael were the operatives on the case. I want to be certain."

Angelica Wallace was small, attractive, frail, barely five feet tall, glasses, with straight chestnut hair down to her shoulders. With her hair arranged, Angelica could pass for a young male teen-ager. Her pale blue eyes would be the giveaway. Alert, relentlessly alert. She quickly looked over Elizabeth's shoulder for a moment, as Michael Zenner came into Mackaye's office.

"It is clearly," said Angelica, with a rich Irish accent, "the layout of a Hawala network, which is capable of moving up to … about $600,000 in a single transaction. Michael?"

"I would agree," he said, looking at the screen between the two women from his 6'2". "But whose network is it, and can they move that much in multiple transactions? Or, much more important, do they *have to move* that much, and why?"

Steele Mackaye stepped alongside. "Please show me the $600K … I have heard of Hawala, of course, but I have never encountered a network. I need a fast education. This may be the motive for one of the killings of Sister Cynthia."

***

Marku, again the invisible postal worker, wearing a partially balding gray-haired wig, walked through the shifting people of the glass-walled lobby of Century Park Plaza, 2029 Century Park East, which looked out on a beautiful green park on one side and the valet parking area on the other. A bank closed the third side of the equilateral lobby. Near five o'clock, there was a general drift from the twenty-six elevators toward the escalator down to the vast parking below. Steele Mackaye Investigations, LLC. One of the three friendly uniformed security guards at the left of the multiple glass entry doors checked her screen, date-stamped and gave him the magnetic card to obtain access to the elevators. Even with his uniform and the confidential parcel that required a personal signature, a secretary would not do, Marku still needed a security card. Not quite as invisible as he had found customary in many American buildings, but close enough.

He flinched slightly when, as he turned away, Marku caught her looking out at the valet parking just outside the main entrance. No postal truck was parked there. He trusted that she would simply conclude that it was parked elsewhere, but the valet parking served both towers, 2029 and 2049. He would avoid her, Marybeth her name tag said, when he returned. He had to maintain his postal guise for the time being.

As he walked unnoticed through the thinning crowd, Marku shook his head. What had suddenly queered his plans was that, without explanation, the money eye had sweetened the deal but had also tightened the timing. Get the CD for $250K, in any condition. Killing as necessary could bring bonuses. Marku would enter the Mackaye offices after hours to search, but now he would first look the situation over, as always before shedding his invisibility. If he found nothing there, then hit the condominium of Sam Milliron in Marina del Rey on Mindanao Way. He had always worked to his own schedule, no client interference, but his options were being squeezed now, and Marku, his face momentarily flushed red, then faded, gritted his teeth. No visible emotion. Never! *Niciodată!* Never!

But he didn't like being squeezed, even for more money!

***

Elizabeth put their move on hold while she, Angelica and Michael gathered around Steele Mackaye's desk to give him a quick tutorial on Hawala networks. Mackaye invited Moana to sit in as well.

Angelica began: "First, I know hawala as my family in Northern Ireland was IRA. I was an innocent invisible little girl, a runner carrying promises.

"But let me begin: as you know in general, hawala is a network that passes promises for money instead of hard cash. It works totally on trust. One mistake or one suspected mishandling will terminate that hawala site ... they are called *hawaladars* ... from the network, either politely or permanently, depending on the function of the network. Because of the depth of trust required, it is usually religious-based and/or ethnic based, principally Asia, Pakistan, India, and Middle East. It is rare, at least from what we have seen, from my own experience, that those boundaries are ever breeched; but in that network" – she pointed at the screen – "the boundaries have been moved in a major way. I became immediately uneasy looking at it."

"Is it legal?" asked Moana.

"Basically, yes," said Elizabeth. "No funds actually cross any borders, only promises. Hawala means 'trust' in Arabic. The system is regularly used by expatriate workers to send money home. It is faster, cheaper and more reliable than the more regulated funds transfers. Usually, there is only a 1% of principal charge for the sending of a few hundred or thousand dollars, rupees, dirham, whatever. The sender can have the currency converted into a local currency at the other end for a slightly higher rate."

"So, how much is sent every year? Any estimates?" asked Moana. "We once had a small setup like this in the islands, according to my father, but then bank funds transfer around the islands became cheaper."

"There are obviously no official numbers as everything is underground," said Michael. "But in the case we finished a couple of months ago, I got an estimate from a financial type that blew me away. Dubai is the largest hawala transaction hub. But the largest in dollars is easily India. Over $550 billion ... almost the GDP of Canada!

"A terrorist, drug dealer, or a money laundering group can move serious money almost without being noticed. The most identifiable aspect of such criminal transactions might be, as Angelica said, crossing the established boundaries." He shrugged. "And even if the various governments try to regulate or tax it, the hawala network would just go further underground, becoming exclusively a criminal activity."

"That CD then could blow off some doors then," said Mackaye. "Any secure transfer system has to have built-in dead ends, pseudonyms, temporary middle men, and what not. That CD network alone could transfer then about $2 billion a year, even, assuming it is jihadist, even with time off for Ramadan."

Elizabeth looked at her iPhone. "Excuse me. HBB business." The phone to her ear, she left the room. It was James Kennedy's private number.

19

"Yes, Mr. Kennedy." Elizabeth glanced over at the glass-doored entrance, glimpsed a few Saturday people passing. A postman carrying a white Priority box hesitated at their door, compared the address on the box, looked around, glanced at her, then moved on. His hesitation was a little long for just confirming an address. His face seemed … too young to have grey hair … and balding. And she was being too suspicious. No reason an older man would not want to appear young. She turned away.

"I apologize for this Saturday intrusion, Ms Vaughn, but I need your answer sooner than Wednesday. About an hour ago, a very excited Melissa told me that HBB may be receiving a major contribution, north of $2.5 million … from the family trust of a close friend. I had nothing to do with their decision, and I hope that Melissa's being my daughter was not a factor, but there it is. Ms Vaughn, I simply cannot allow my friend's money to be … to be, well, endangered."

"I can be at HBB on Monday morning, Mr. Kennedy. We should be reasonably moved in by the end of Sunday. I have some questions about their website to start the conversation. I will not be revealing either my PI status, or your involvement."

"How will you approach Melissa? She will nail any phoniness, believe me."

Elizabeth smiled. She was looking forward to meeting the Mighty Melissa. "I will be a screen-writer doing preliminary research work for a documentary on new rehabilitation techniques for ex-cons and parolees. I am looking for one or two organizations to focus on. My producer has won awards for his documentary work … including prisoner rehabilitation. He is aware of the confidentiality of my work."

"Brilliant, Ms Vaughan! I would never have thought of that. I doubt Melissa would see anything amiss. Please keep me informed as you feel appropriate. Please use this phone number. And I will start the clock as of now."

"I will call you on Wednesday, Mr. Kennedy, after I have a couple of days of digging in place. And thank you for your generosity." She caught the postal worker walking by again, without the box, slowing momentarily at the Mackaye door then moving on, his head quickly averted. Elizabeth, curious, walked to the door, pushed it open a couple of inches to look after him. The black granite floored corridor was empty of Saturday traffic. Silent.

He had vanished!

***

Steele Mackaye nodded to Elizabeth's observation. Homeless had returned. "I'll get Toni on board. He clearly is going to hit this office after hours to search for the CD. If just killing was all he was being paid for, then he could have gotten us all. He didn't find the CD at Sister Cynthia's sanctum, and didn't find her home in time to search there. Since he could not know of the material in her Bible, then the fact he's here says someone told him the CD is here. He certainly isn't waiting for the cop at Cynthia's door to be removed. Someone must have leaked somehow.

"Anyway, we can probably get him for b-and-e if nothing else", said Mackaye. "Thanks, Elizabeth, for your sharp eyes."

She laughed. "After Kennedy called me brilliant for the screenwriter cover, I owed you. See you Sunday afternoon?"

"Probably. I have some work to get done that has nothing to do with Cynthia. But I need to get to Toni first."

***

The corridor was empty, all the offices dark, each with only one night-light on. Sergeant Encarna Reynoso, dressed as a cleaning woman slowly pushed the large cart loaded with cleaning fluids, brushes, a mop, a pile of toilet paper rolls. Her Glock 23 was in the bag at her waist holding small brushes. Officer Paco Garcia carried a vacuum cleaner strapped to his back pushing the chrome and red cleaning head, his Glock 17 wedged between the cleaner and the small of his back. Officer Jose Apostol, borrowed from SWAT for the evening, was pushing a cart with two large trash canisters with his night stick hidden between them and his S&W 1911 .45 under his cleaner's jacket in a quick draw holster.

No white cops could be used for the upstairs stakeout. They would be downstairs at each of the six service elevators with four more discretely covering the elevator complex in the lobby. 26 elevators, but only two exits from the complex.

Three Hispanic cleaners would work the Mackaye floor. Three would enter the Mackaye office and, after a surface clean, emptying waste baskets and such, three would come out, after leaving Detective Rodriguez behind.

Crouched in a trash container, Toni would be the first line if Homeless hit the Mackaye office tonight. If she couldn't contain him, in public terminology … or, nail the bastard, in cop-speak … she had solid backup. Homeless was not vanishing tonight except into the back-seat of a black-and-white with all lights flashing.

She smiled recalling Steele's suggestion. Even if somehow Homeless got away, he was still going to have interesting problems.

***

Marku didn't like the looker on the cell who had been standing in the Mackaye reception area. He should have moved quicker, but still, the odds were more than on his side with his invisibility still firmly in place. He stood and stretched. Now wearing a shirt that claimed he was from an electrical supply house with a red-haired wig, the hair crew-cut. His knife in place, and, tonight, a small .38 snub-nose in the small of his back. The gun was a last resort. He had had to use a gun before only once, and had no choice then. The squeeze ... damnit. He was being forced into doing stupid things if he wasn't very careful.

It was 9:30, time to check. A narrow crack at the door of the storage closet revealed the three cleaners exiting the last office at the end of the corridor and heading toward the service elevator around the corner to move up to the next floor. Once they were out of sight, he would give them fifteen minutes to allow for their forgetting anything. They were the same three he had watched come onto the floor over two hours ago. He felt uneasy. If the looker had somehow made him, odds were the cleaners were cops. Three Mex cops up here and a bunch of whites down below. But no one would expect him to be here. To the cops, there was no way he could know of the CD. But cops or not, he had to move. The squeeze ... and the fact that the CD may be moved, leaving him to wait again for its location, which could queer his contact. He had to move.

Marku carried a leather bag with pliers and various rolls of electrical tape hanging on it. He moved rapidly, but not too fast, never out of character. It was too easy to outrun invisibility. Marku swore silently. He would not let the squeeze queer his setup at the last minute.

Mackaye. Marku took his picks from the bag, a
minute on one lock at the bottom of the glass door, then
another minute on the second at the top. A night light was on
over the entrance to a conference room. He would start with
the biggest office, which would be Mackaye's. If the CD was
here, odds were it would be somewhere in that office.

Identifying Mackaye, or Milliron, had been the easiest
step ... Marku had recognized him from the dust jacket of his
latest book, then a bit of internet browsing had brought all the
rest. Seeing him at the blonde whore's sanctum and later at
her home fixed him as a problem to be solved. If the police
had the CD, he had no chance. The money eye had another
approach for that. Then he would just kill the two, take the
bonus money and move on. But ...

Boxes piled in various offices. Clearly not Mackaye.
The red door next to the conference room. Mackaye? Yes!
Marku moved quickly to the desk. All the drawers were
locked. He picked the central drawer, which also unlocked
the top drawers on each side.

Nothing in the top drawers. A moment to pick the two
right side drawers. Nothing. The two left. He pulled out a
locked wooden storage case from the bottom drawer. A
combo lock. No time for playing with combinations. Using a

rubber mallet, he drove a steel wedge into the back of the box. A hard downward lunge, and the box split open. The CD was there! He quickly scanned it for the secret UV markings with his smart phone. They were there. Marku was holding $250K in his hand! He slid the disc and transparent cover into his shirt, and began to move toward the door.

What? Something … an odd noise. His knife instantly in his hand, Marku gently pulled the red door open.

The lights came on!

"Don't move an inch!" shouted Toni. "I'll take your head off! Turn toward me very slowly with your arms spread away from your body! Down! Get down on your knees!"

Marku turned slowly to see a Mex female cop in a cleaners getup with a cocked Glock 23 held in the prescribed manner. Her eyes were filled with hate. No ear plugs. She couldn't call for backup until he was cuffed. Marku nodded as he continued to turn slowly, spreading his arms. His body was moving slowly, but his left hand was instantaneous. She had no time to react as the knife slammed deep into her chest, except to gasp in surprise. He rolled to one side to dodge her one shot that ricocheted off the floor to crack the glass of the door as she fell forward. Marku quickly pushed up from the floor, took two steps, kicked the bitch's face in. He was at the door in three strides, his invisibility gone. But $250K in his pocket!

20

Stunned, Steele Mackaye listened as Miles Harper unloaded his rage. Harper's call at nine in the morning had immediately shattered his day. Toni on life support, massive injuries to her face and neck. Her odds were, according to Harper quoting the surgeon in charge, less than 50-50.

"Don't bother with the hospital, Steele, Toni won't know you, and the doctors won't let anyone near her, and neither will the squad of pissed-off cops I have guarding the doors. Jesus, after everything in place, and it goes so wrong!" Harper's angry voice was finally beginning to calm. "We have to get this bastard, have to. You called it right, Steele, he knew the CD was there, which raises a lot of other questions for us, like where the hell did his input come from?"

"Where was her backup?"

"The floor backup was just around the corner about only forty-fifty feet away waiting. It was Apostol from SWAT who smelled something wrong. He thought he heard a shot. He ran for your office without Toni calling in backup. He saved her life ... at least so far. I owe him big time. Only Toni can tell us what actually happened. But the damned perp disappeared again. We had the tower surrounded within minutes, had two squads in the parking area under the building ... nothing, Steele, nothing! Like the bastard was never even there." The line went dead.

Mackaye called Moana.

***

Marku waited as the money eye slid the CD into the computer. The UV markings had checked out. He could almost feel the cash in his fingers. He had collected on the $50K target.

"What the shit is this?" exploded the money eye, a Qatari professor of Muslim history at UC San Diego, with a number of non-academic contacts.

Marku went cold inside when he saw the message:

This CD was stolen from the offices of Steele Mackaye Investigations, LLC.

Shame on you.

***

Elizabeth needed a way to hit Melissa with fraud without bringing in her father … assuming, naturally, that she was successful in discovering the alleged embezzlement.

Melissa's love affair was not a part of her PI agenda. Papa will just have to deal with that himself.

The Form 990's showed an increase of funding from the initial donations three years ago from two east-coast foundations of $300,000. A good start. The original Executive Director had done a great job pitching HBB. It hadn't been Melissa as she joined HBB a year later, as Director, then became Executive Director within two months. The original Executive Director/pitchman was gone for some undisclosed reason. The funding had grown to $850 thousand at the end of the second year, and $1.2 million as of three months ago, the end of their third fiscal year. HBB, for each of its fiscal years, had entered "no" on Line 5, Section 6 of the 990, on "diversions". Any diversion, theft or embezzlement, had to be greater than $250,000 or 5% of the organization's annual gross receipts or assets to require a "yes" entry with an explanation entered a few pages later. The IRS diversion requirement had been in place since 2008.

So, James Kennedy says his daughter is being stolen blind, while Melissa is telling the IRS that everything is fine. Elizabeth smiled. She was looking forward to their Monday morning. She had already sent an e-mail to Melissa regarding her documentary project, asking to drop by for an initial conversation. She had received an immediate e-mailed yes.

21

Marku had passed through the gate at Mackaye's condo complex without issue. The security was so lax, he could have just walked in by going around the backside of the guard shack while the one guard at the gate was dealing with a visitor, but do it the right way, right up to the very last minute. Step out of the invisible only for the kill, then back in. It wasn't a fire drill, no rush. But today, he would get Mackaye, CD or not. As he told the money eye, Mackaye he would do for free, and if it was there, get the genuine CD.

Marku had walked around the block at around nine, left for a nearby Peet's, then walked it again at ten. No obvious signs of any undercover cops. All the parked cars on the street were either empty or clearly local, or he had watched people come out of apartments and condos to drive them away or to pull up. He had used a story of a relative maybe getting the wrong address, and had they seen any strange cars cruising the street like looking for an address. All the helpful sympathetic answers were no.

Marku had told the guard he was going into Building A, Mackaye's building, keeping everything legitimate for the time. He was wearing the partially balding gray wig again, his suit a bit rumpled, his glasses dark. He was an antique book dealer bringing some books for a resident of Building A. The resident was away for a brief time, he explained to the guard, but he had been asked by his client if he would leave the briefcase at his door. He would be leaving immediately thereafter. The guard waved him through …almost too quickly. After last night, cops had to be everywhere, probably over there clipping the hedges, and, maybe, waiting up on the third floor. After doing Mackaye, maybe he could take one or two of them.

As the man with briefcase passed the guard shack, Paco Garcia put down his hedge clippers. He was dressed as a workman along with several legitimate workers in the crew. "Homeless is here," he whispered into his cell. The guard at the gate was Officer Jimmy Lawrence. Mackaye had given him the details of all the disguises used thus far by Homeless. When Lawrence confirmed the disguise, Garcia picked up his clippers, and began to walk rapidly toward Building A. He keyed Harper's phone. The off-site backup would be in place in only three or four minutes.

Mackaye was on the third floor of a three story, open architecture gray and white building. Ten condos on each floor were arranged around an open courtyard filled with flowers and palms on the first floor. Marku climbed the stairs. No one was walking on the first two floors. He saw a pudgy Mex cleaning woman carrying a bucket walking away from him toward Mackaye's end of the balcony that encircled the flower garden down below. She continued past the end toward another condo opposite Mackaye, then disappeared onto the tiled entrance. No problem. Marku continued past Mackaye's door, circled all around the balcony. No one seemed home, though a wheel-chair was on one of the brownish-red tiled entrances. He continued back to Mackaye's door. No cops, fake or otherwise.

He gently tried Mackaye's door. It was unlocked. Marku pushed it open and stepped in, locking the door behind him. No interruptions.

"Marta, the spare room doesn't need cleaning this week," called out Mackaye.

Marku continued down the hallway. The voice had come from a room ahead to the left, otherwise the place was silent. The condo was open up to a soaring ceiling with an empty loft walled with filled bookcases up to the right. No one around. Clearly Mackaye expected the cleaning woman to return. She would have to ring the doorbell to get in. No problem.

Marku assumed that Mackaye would expect him to come. The prod of the humiliating CD message would be too great to ignore. No problem. He had a way out even with police back-up in place.

His knife ready in his left hand, Marku turned the corner as Mackaye, in a white terry bathrobe, his back to him, started to turn, the knife already sped on its way.

***

"Excellent work, Moana," said Steele Mackaye. Homeless was laid out on the floor, his head oozing blood onto the polished parquet floor. Mackaye dropped the block of wood with the knife embedded on a chair. With Toni's experience, he had had the block under his robe over his heart. Homeless, it seemed, never missed.

Moana, dressed as a cleaning woman with extra padding around her torso and gray highlights in her black hair, held a bloody black and red Mo'orea war club in her hand. She had swung it as her father, who, with no sons, had taught her to be a warrior: putting her body into the swing, driving the carved head of the club from her hips and back, toward the base of the skull from behind, for the temple from in front. Then step back, ready to swing again, which she had done. Two strikes had taken Homeless down.

"He never saw me, Boss. Walked right by me like I didn't exist … like I was invisible. I waited, as you said, until he entered your condo so I didn't crack the wrong head." She flashed a glorious smile. "Thanks for trusting me, Boss. My father would be proud of his warrior-child."

Mackaye straightened up from securing plastic ties around the wrists and ankles of Homeless. He could hear Harper and his men coming down the hallway. Once Mackaye had heard his condo door open, he had pressed the speed dial for Harper.

When Harper, backed by three uniforms, appeared, he broke into a wide grin. When he noted the bloody war club in Moana's hand, his grin became wider. Harper had resisted Mackaye's decision to have Moana as his backup, with cops at least five minutes away; but now he stepped toward her his hand outstretched. "Moana, I want you on my side any time bull-crap hits the fan."

She laughed. "So long as you give me at least five minutes notice, Lieutenant, to fix my hair, I will be there."

At Harper's direction, the uniforms moved to pick up Homeless, but paused as Mackaye was down removing the wig and the whiskers to see what Homeless really looked like.

My God, Mackaye had seen Homeless before … but where … where?

22

A very stylized *Hope Beyond Bars* in gold, scarlet and blue sprawled across the glass wall of the office on the third floor that overlooked 4th Street, in downtown Santa Monica. Inside the office four men, three black and one Asian with two white women all dressed as if for cleaning out a garage were gathered in casual conversation holding Starbucks cups sitting on red leather chairs and sofa at one side. A receptionist in washed and torn jeans and black droopy sweater off one shoulder was typing intensely at the desk-top computer. Elizabeth pushed the door open. She was dressed in black designer jeans with a black ribbed silk blouse and running shoes. Not quite PI-formal.

***

"Please come in, Ms Vaughn, I'm Melissa Kennedy." She had appeared almost instantly as though the receptionist's call was a starter's gun. After a brief handshake, Elizabeth followed the young attractive though over-weight woman. She wore a striped jacket and black skirt with a white open-neck business shirt. The fingernails on her right hand were bitten raw.

There were no windows in Melissa's office. To the left, the wall had six gold-framed awards of some kind hanging, while behind Melissa's long and littered black-topped steel desk was her Harvard degree with a large color photo of her alone at her graduation. To the right, as Elizabeth settled into a comfortable deep blue leather chair were multiple mixed photos of b/w and color of various smiling and grinning people of varying ages.

Melissa looked up from Elizabeth's business card. "You are with Mendelsson Productions? They have done some very good things."

"No," said Elizabeth, "I am an independent contractor working on spec. Once my research has solidified, decisions made, and my doc treatment in place, basically my story arc, then I sit down with Eric and pitch like hell." She grinned. "But I eat well. I have done this more than once, but Eric is particularly interested in the ex-con angle since he did a doc on rehabilitation about six years ago. Won some prizes, which is always nice, but the distys were turned off by the pessimistic tone of the work."

Melissa sipped her grande. "What are you looking for?" She flashed the business card. "May I keep this?"

"Of course." Elizabeth opened her tablet. "According to your website, your approach is to trust, establish high expectation, and give the men and women training for solid work to do, not just busy-work to pretend with, to help them get their feet moving in the right direction. Have I said that about right?"

Melissa smiled and nodded. "Trust is the key."

"Do they have to earn it … or do you grant it upfront?"

"In our view, Elizabeth, it must be upfront. You don't have months to prove trust with these people. I've seen in some prior experience, ex-cons and parolees going off the tracks while waiting to get into real work.

"One thing here that you will find to be different is that the organizational chart is largely filled by the people we are here to help. That has stymied some foundations and donors, but they are coming around. We have a $2.5 million donation from a private foundation on the horizon that will enable us do many other things faster."

"Melissa, could I get a copy of the org chart and a tour, so I can begin to carve out areas for a set of first pass interviews. I have a tight schedule to get my pitch honed and in front of Eric when he finishes his Ten Commandments documentary."

"Ten Commandments? He's carving stone tablets?" she laughed. Melissa slid an org chart across the desk. "I'll ask Dieter to give you our dollar tour."

"One last thing, Melissa, how does HBB, if I can use that expression, define success? Not total organizational success, but body by body success." Fully expecting a smartass response, Elizabeth was pleasantly surprised.

Melissa pursed her lips. "Given realities of time and money, HBB can only take things so far. So if one of our clients, as we call the men and women we support, has been out of police trouble for one year *and* is fully employed for at least nine months of that year, then HBB can rightly take some credit, Our focus is not how many people we can run through those doors out there, but how many have crossed that line I described."

"What is your score, after three years?"

"Twelve." Melissa beat her right fist lightly on her desk. "Just twelve, out of 116 clients. Our first year was wasted in experiments, with maybe only one or two clients making it. Our objective this fiscal year is to get our batting average up to 20%. I think we can do it. Maybe your documentary could help."

As Elizabeth turned to the knock on the office door, she asked, "May I ask, what was your major at Harvard?"

"Chinese Literature."

"You mean like Dream of the Red Chamber and Cases of Judge Bao, or more specialized?"

Melissa's jaw dropped slightly. "I focused on the Classics, translated texts. My Chinese capability is limited."

Elizabeth grinned. "So is mine."

23

"So, Dieter, what crime did you commit and are you parolee or ex-con? Please excuse my bluntness, but I want to get a handle on HBB as quickly as I can." Clearly Dieter was the man who so disturbed James Kennedy.

Dieter Jaeger, a tall blue-eyed blonde from Munich, grinned. "I look criminal?" He had spoken with a modest German accent when they met, his handshake had been gentle, not macho.

"Melissa was emphatic that clients were also a part of the organization, so I bet on your criminal status."

As he guided her across the reception room with the four men and two women still emptying their Starbucks cups, Dieter whispered, "I don't really like that name and its gaudy display on the doors. But Melissa loves it." He shrugged. "But to your question, I was and am a car thief. And a very good one, if I might brag a bit. I am on parole, so my movements are tracked somewhat, and I have been involved with HBB for almost eight months now. And I prize Melissa's trust ..."

As he opened a door that revealed a long white-and-black carpeted corridor, Elizabeth asked, "So what queered your last pick-up that pulled you back into prison?"

"A silly accident, that would take too much of your time to describe. I have three more years to finish my sentence. Here," he said, knocking against the doorframe, "let me introduce the man who handles our purchasing and contracts, George Jenness."

Jenness stood as Dieter explained Elizabeth's presence. He reached out to grip her hand with a single firm shake, then said, as he resumed his chair, "How may I help, Ms Vaughn?" The negative vibes between Dieter and George were instant and obvious.

"I am not sure yet, Mr. Jenness, I am just on an introductory tour." A few pleasantries and the tour continued meeting Carly Magnuson, head of training, who was just leaving to supervise two hours of off-campus training, and John Scott, head of Donor Interface, or as John had grinned,

"The focused wining and dining." They finished at Dieter's office, the walls covered with photos of cars of all types.

"I need to understand your duties, Dieter. George purchases and …"

"I pay the bills. I can tell from your expression, your question is how can Melissa have George, a free-man, as we call it, do the buying, while I, a parolee, actually sign the checks."

Elizabeth nodded.

"Because that's the way she set it up. Real trust and real duties. My parole officer, a delightful woman named Marian, was even more astonished and spent time with Melissa to be sure she correctly understood the arrangement."

"That Black Ford Focus there in the corner. All the other photos are of serious high dollar cars, why that one. Your first steal?"

Dieter laughed. "Excellent insight, Elizabeth, but no. When I escaped from my last prison, I stole the Warden's car for my getaway. The lot was full so I had my choice, but I couldn't pass up the Warden's Ford."

Elizabeth laughed. "A nice touch of style. So then you drove away, the accident happened and here you are." She cocked her head, waiting.

"Exactly."

"So you pay whatever invoices that George sends you, is that the play?"

"Yes."

"And who tells him what to buy. Melissa, certainly, but who else?"

"Carly, primarily," he said. "We have brochures, other printed goods, contract payments."

"Do you use just one bank? I don't know why I ask that, just grist for my mill."

"We actually use two banks. But why, you'll have to ask Melissa. She sets up which checks I sign for which type of invoice."

"Great. Is there an unused office I could use to sort things out … get my targets lined up. And I would like to interview two or three clients at various stages of their experience with HBB, if that can be arranged today."

24

Elizabeth shuffled through her notes as Jim brought her his specialty, a rabbit-sausage, Swiss cheese and dried morel omelet, crisp hash browns, with two cinnamon biscuits standing guard. With their favorite Sauvignon Blanc, naturally. She ate in her home office while he ate in the kitchen. After half an hour, Jim came in with two coffee cups, sat down, and said, "So, my beautiful detective, throw it all at me."

Elizabeth laughed softly. He was always there when she needed him. "Something smells, Jim. I told you about James Kennedy's two concerns. And Dieter is a very attractive man, so Melissa's interest is natural, if, given the situation, a little off-base. But that's not my problem, I thought, but now maybe it is a part."

"Everyone I met, including three new clients just released on parole, seem really committed to the program. This is not just an expensive feel-good game that Melissa is playing. She wants to go national within two more years, with maybe $50 million in revenues – with zero help from her 'over-rich' Dad as she puts it.

"I walked all the offices," she said, "the conference rooms, two of them, and the back-lot, as they all call it, the inventory and storage room." She put her cup down. "But Jim, something doesn't fit just right. It's not just the potential embezzlement that Kennedy is upset about, there is something else there. The HBB programs read as innovative and, just maybe, effective … "

"Sounds like Jenness and Jaeger are off track. The free-man and the con. Did Jenness show any special regard for the Mighty Melissa? Romantic interest, to be specific."

"A little, but not beyond a little office yearning, it seemed. But there is no doubt about their friction." She shrugged. "I'm not going to get much sleep tonight. I looked on this as a quick 3-4 day service to a major client. It is something else, something I heard. "

"Well, I'm happy to hear that Steele nailed the bad guy without your having to get involved," said Jim. "It's one thing to track money-laundering, then step out of the way for the cops; but very much another to take down killers."

***

Eric confirmed that Melissa had called and had requested a physical description. "A very tight woman, Elizabeth. I'd be careful with her. Reminds me of a producer I once worked for. Turned out he was playing a tight game and didn't want certain people to see it." He coughed. "Don't take me too seriously on that. I'm probably just looking the wrong way."

***

Elizabeth listened as the offices emptied and the place grew quiet. Melissa had left for a donor meeting at three and wasn't coming back. Dieter was out for the day at the parole office. George was the last to go.

"Got your story together, yet, Ms Vaughn?" he asked, leaning against the doorframe. He would not call her Elizabeth.

"It is starting to take shape, Mr. Jenness. Some interesting people, both pro and con, to coin a phrase."

He grinned, waved and left.

All the office doors, but hers, were locked. Elizabeth picked Dieter's lock quickly. He had left a stack of invoices in his in-basket. She wanted to look at the vendors without having to ask anyone … and get out before the cleaners arrived.

She flipped quickly through the invoices with packing slips stapled to them arranged for those vendors offering discounts for early payments. A random comparison showed the packing slip matched the invoice. But then, she turned back. A-1 printing supplies. Printer inks, paper, other stuff, all discount. But, she pulled the other A-1 invoice she had come across. One was to be paid early, the other later. Routine misplacement … maybe. She thumbed deeper in the early and late piles. Not just A-1, but two other vendors. She glanced over the packing slips. Quantities and pricing matched the invoice. Oh, crap! The date on one packing slip was next week! The invoice was for $1,250 for computer supplies without detail … while on the other invoice each quantity was broken down by item. The vendor Kola, Corporation, Ventura, had come up regularly in her flip through. She had seen this pattern before on earlier cases. The routine used as a cover. Was Kola in on the scam? Each of the earlier clients who had experienced this type of embezzlement, had resolved the issue by requiring two signatures on checks. But it wasn't always just the money.

***

Late Wednesday afternoon, James Kennedy's face was ashen as Elizabeth outlined what she had found. "It may be Dieter or George, or both working together using their apparent animosity as cover," she said." If HBB were national then money could be spread everywhere, and/or illegal stuff like drugs could be moved under the invoices. Most NPO's don't have the staff or the expertise to cover everything.

"Many NPO's who discover something like this, just ask the people to leave and then say nothing, even to the IRS, to avoid endangering their donor base. Oftentimes, the embezzler will excuse their theft calling it a temporary loan, promising to repay everything. At which point after a token payment or two, they disappear."

Kennedy cradled his head between his hands. He was silent for several minutes. Finally he looked up, glanced out at the lowering sun. "You have done as I asked. And done it well and quickly. I hesitate to ask more, particularly as you have a firm to run yourself." He leaned back in his chair. "What can you suggest, Ms Vaughn?"

"If I go back," said Elizabeth, "I have perhaps 3-4 days at the end of which with my cover story, I must say that my producer has decided against my project, and thank Melissa for her time. Then come away with whatever I've found which may not be enough on which to take action. Or," she smiled, "I have to write a screenplay and take it all the way till conclusive action can be taken. But I can't do that. I cannot make that commitment.

"However, I have an operative who is just off a difficult case and needs some slow time. Her name is Angelica Wallace. She will be my replacement, while I have been asked by the producer to help with another project. I could drop by on occasion to maintain a presence. But," she emphasized, "regardless, at some specific point, soon, Melissa must take action or she will lose everything, IRS or not." Elizabeth tapped the table. "And, Mr. Kennedy, we still need to determine if the activity is just to take money from HBB, or if it is something more … more threatening. Angelica will be looking for that."

"You might remind your daughter of the proverb from the Ming Dynasty: *Try to save a dead horse as if it is still alive.*"

25

The questions to Stephen Minch following his lecture in the backroom of the Erdnase Café were finally wrapping up. After about a fifteen minute break, Stephen would be inscribing copies of his *Book of Lost Secrets*. A smiling bearded man of slight build with bright eyes of an uncertain blue behind glasses, Stephen settled onto the chair next to Moana.

"Such marvelous revelations, Stephen," she smiled. "With a feathered cloak, no shoes or pants, and some drumming in the background, you would be almost at home in the marae ahu o Mahine on my island."

Replacing his glass of pinot noir, Stephen grinned. "What is a marae, and why the strip-tease?"

Her coquettish smile brought a grin to Minch's face. "The gods are jealous creatures," she said. "They demand that you have nothing between you and them; and a marae is an ancient temple, the subject of a project that the Boss and I are working on with the help of the Bishop Museum in Honolulu."

"I would like to learn more of marae," said Minch. "Are copies of your doctoral thesis available for an enquiring book publisher?"

Leaning closer as the mob noise seemed to expand, Moana raised an eyebrow. "You mean through your Hermetic Press? There wouldn't be a large enough market … would there?"

"Let's talk about it."

Mackaye reached his hand across the table. "Just great, Stephen. I was taking notes as fast as I could. I could use a couple of your lines in the short story I have in progress. Okay?

"And I assume you have a deal with Bat for a DVD of tonight's lecture?"

Stephen raised his glass. "Yes to both of your questions."

Masterson pushed his way to the table. "Stephen, enough relaxing. Time to meet your fans, and it is my turn for the chair next to Moana." The table laughter was lost in the almost deafening jumble of voices interspersed with sounds like ripping cabbage, the sound of decks of cards shuffling again and again. "And the off-site portion we can do in the office in back of the magic shop whenever you're ready." Stephen nodded and started elbowing his way toward the table stacked with copies of his book.

"A dynamite evening, Bat," said Mackaye. "You book a return yet?"

Bat swallowed, finishing his beer. "After tonight's performance, I won't be able to afford him. It was great." He turned to Moana who was watching the movements of the crowd, her eyes seeming to float over them. "You're seeing something that the rest of us are missing, Moana. What is it?"

Moana sat back into her chair. "I was just thinking of Paul Gauguin's three questions:

Who are we?

Where have we come from?

Where are we going?

"The people there in their movements create a special presence, almost an urgency that is beyond the fun of tonight. They remind me of the flourishing roaring flames of the celebratory fires on my island. Always changing, greater, smaller, but always …always … reaching for the gods." Her half-smile was gentle. "My great-grandfather knew Gauguin, briefly." She looked over at Mackaye. "Boss, you need to have Paul Gauguin in one of your stories." Moana turned back to Bat, her broad smile lighting her face, and his as well. "I'm just enjoying the celebration, Bat."

With Toni out of immediate danger, with her continuing recovery, both Steele and Moana could simply enjoy the evening with their only mutual concern an irate publisher. Or so it seemed.

27

His head still aching, Marku Antonescu looked out the small window of his cell. An LA County Sheriff's black and white rolled by below. Marku only smiled, a small smile. If he felt the police anywhere close to him again, he would vanish again, but not without *plata lor diavolul!* ... their paying the devil! And he would get out. No jail had ever held him. And he would get Mackaye. No one had ever escaped his hands. And the money-eye's contact had told him who had clubbed him that night. He would also visit the Polynesian woman.

She would feel his *ciocanel* ... his hammer

Other Books by Barry H. Wiley

The *Adventures in Second Sight* Series

Set in the turbulent final decade of the 19th century, *Adventures in Second Sight* tells of the adventurous life of Kyame Piddington as she encounters bank robbers, killers, con men, Jadoo-wallahs, and the hatchet men of the Bing On tong as beginning at age eleven she travels the American West with her father as The Impossible Piddingtons … and the consistent rejection by polite society because Kyame is only a theatre girl.

Kyame's later travels take her beyond America to England, France, Hawaii and the islands of the South Seas during which she encounters historical personages as Paul Gauguin; the Prince of Wales; Queen Victoria; the greatest American mesmerist, J. W. Cadwell; British Prime Minister,

Lord Salisbury; and others, lesser known, but very much historically real.

Book 1, *Revelations of the Impossible Piddingtons.*
http://amazon.com/dp/B003VP9W6E

It is1890-95. "Kyame seems a girl ready for her dragon tattoo ...," according to the Kirkus Media. Continuing, Kirkus says, "Wiley deftly renders the period atmosphere, attitudes, action and dialogue ... Kyame could develop a loyal following of readers of all ages and sexes ..." And regarding the novel, Kirkus describes it as, "A magical concept and a miraculous heroine keep the pages turning ..." Published 2010.

Book 2, *The Shadow of the Tiger.*
http://amazon.com/dp/B00LP287CK

It is 1896. All the British intelligence agents in Southern France have been killed. Even their replacements are murdered within a few days of their appearing. Lord Salisbury, British Prime

Minister, appeals to President Grover Cleveland for assistance. With no American intelligence presence in Europe, Cleveland must turn to a unique informal group called the Anglo-Oriental Insurance Co. that reports to Richard Olney, his Secretary of State. Though seventeen, only Kyame Piddington has the unique skills needed to confront N, the Imperial German Intelligence Service, as Kaiser Wilhelm II pushes to control the Mediterranean Sea and threaten British control of the Suez Canal. Kyame must utilize all of her strange skills, including the yellow ruhmal of the Thuggee cult, in her battle to understand and stop the German threat. Kyame also encounters a young Frenchman who captures her heart only to disappear. Published 2014.

Book 3 **Pi Ying Xi** *The Shadow Play.* Set in 1897 in San Francisco, Honolulu, Cairo, and Tahiti. To be released in 2015.

The Thought Reading Craze, McFarland, 2012. A non-fiction study of the intense search by scientists, academics and others to establish telepathy as a fact of human nature and perhaps the first scientific proof of life-after-death. The book also tells the story of the men, woman and, occasionally, children who so successfully hoaxed the scientists; as well as the parallel story of the creation of the one-man minding act one Monday morning in 1873 in a Chicago saloon. The stage performers used the scientists to gain public credit, while the scientists used the performers to maintain public interest. In the end, the performers gained and lost fortunes, while the scientists gained and lost reputations. Winner of the 2013 Christopher Literary Award.

The Thought Reader Craze is available on Amazon, Barnes & Noble, and the McFarland website in both print and e-book formats.

***The Indescribable Phenomenon: the life and
mysteries of Anna Eva Fay***, Hermetic Press, 2005.
The biography of the woman whom, in 1909,
magician Harry Houdini called, "the greatest female
mystifier". In 1875 Annie was publicly acclaimed
by scientists and psychical researchers in Great
Britain as a genuine psychic, capable of exerting a
"non-human force at a distance"; while in 1877,
detective Allan Pinkerton called her, "... a woman
possessing a terribly fascinating power and capable
of any devilish human accomplishment."

Raised in conditions of near slavery in
northeastern Ohio, five feet tall, blonde, blue-eyed,
Annie Fay was the quintessential con woman.
Though a fake, she became celebrated as one of the
premier spirit mediums of her day; when the profits
from her spirits began to fade, in 1894 Annie went
on the vaudeville stage doing what she had been
doing in the séance room. She stole the mindreading
act of magician Samri S. Baldwin to fill out her act,

and became celebrated as a greater showman than Houdini himself. Baldwin himself said publicly that she performed the act better than he did. When Anna Eva Fay died in 1927, she was eulogized in the New York *Times*. The biography was considered for a film by Walden Media, but the project never moved ahead. Available on Amazon, and from the publisher, Hermetic Press in Seattle, WA www.hermeticpress.com

A Spirit of Fraud. Set in 1876. A British occult Brotherhood under the apparent direction of the Archangel Uriel plans to seize defenseless America in the waning months of the Grant administration. Only the celebrated spirit medium, Annie Eva Fay, detects the threatening presence of Uriel's minions. Gaining the help of the Pinkertons, Annie moves to stop the Brotherhood. But Annie's spirits are all fake. Is the Archangel a fake as well? And will there be time enough for Annie to learn the truth? The novel was reviewed October, 2014, on *Kings River Life Magazine* (www.kingsriverlife.com) with a comparison to *The DaVinci Code.*

A Spirit of Fraud is distributed through Smashwords to Kobo, Barnes & Noble, and Apple iBookstore.

Beyond The Tempest, a sorcerous tale of Bermuda. Bermuda. Pink sand, exotic beauty, mysterious history, a three billion dollar national debt, and a per capita murder rate twice that of New York even with the most draconian gun control law in the Western world: Ten years in prison without parole for possession of any gun, or any part of a gun. In *Beyond The Tempest,* the real Bermuda is a principal character in the novel, not simply a tourist backdrop.

Set in contemporary times, the novel tells the story of mentalist and former physicist, Kaarin Larsson, who is booked at the last minute into a venture capital conference in Bermuda to replace Tony DiMarco, celebrated memory expert who has been murdered twice, shot with a .32 and a .41 magnum at the same time in a deserted Bermuda cemetery. DiMarco's killers thus were risking hard time just holding the guns. But why two killers?

Kaarin is attacked by two killers her first night in Bermuda, one with the .41 and one with a knife. She knows no one in Bermuda – why her?

Together with Inspector Keith Haggard of the Bermuda Police Service, she searches for answers. Why are her friends Serreta and Sugar Alberts, magicians currently performing at the Pink Sands in Bermuda, also targeted?

But the constant underlying question that torments her nights, and her unguarded moments: is she human?

Note: Research for *Beyond The Tempest* included interviewing the Bermuda Commissioner of Police, which resulted in his assigning an officer to show Bermuda as the police see it -- a remarkably fascinating afternoon in paradise.

Beyond The Tempest is distributed through Smashwords to Barnes & Noble, Kobo, and Apple iBookstore.

For more information on the stories and books of Barry H. Wiley visit his website at www.creatorofmysteriousstories.com. Follow his Author's Page and his blog "Plotting the Impossible" on Goodreads.

www.ingramcontent.com/pod-product-compliance
Lightning Source LLC
Chambersburg PA
CBHW071238130626
46556CB00003B/1061